A VANE AND ROC ORIGIN STORY

DARK & DARKER STILL

USA TODAY BESTSELLING AUTHOR

NIKKI ST. CROWE

Cover Design by Cass at Opulent Designs

CONTENT WARNING

Graphic language, violence, gore, abusive parent, talk of suicide, alluding to sexual assault, graphic sexual content, blood drinking, war, displacement, death of family

For a more comprehensive list of all of Nikki's work, please visit her website or scan the QR code below.

https://www.nikkistcrowe.com/content-warnings

SCAN ME

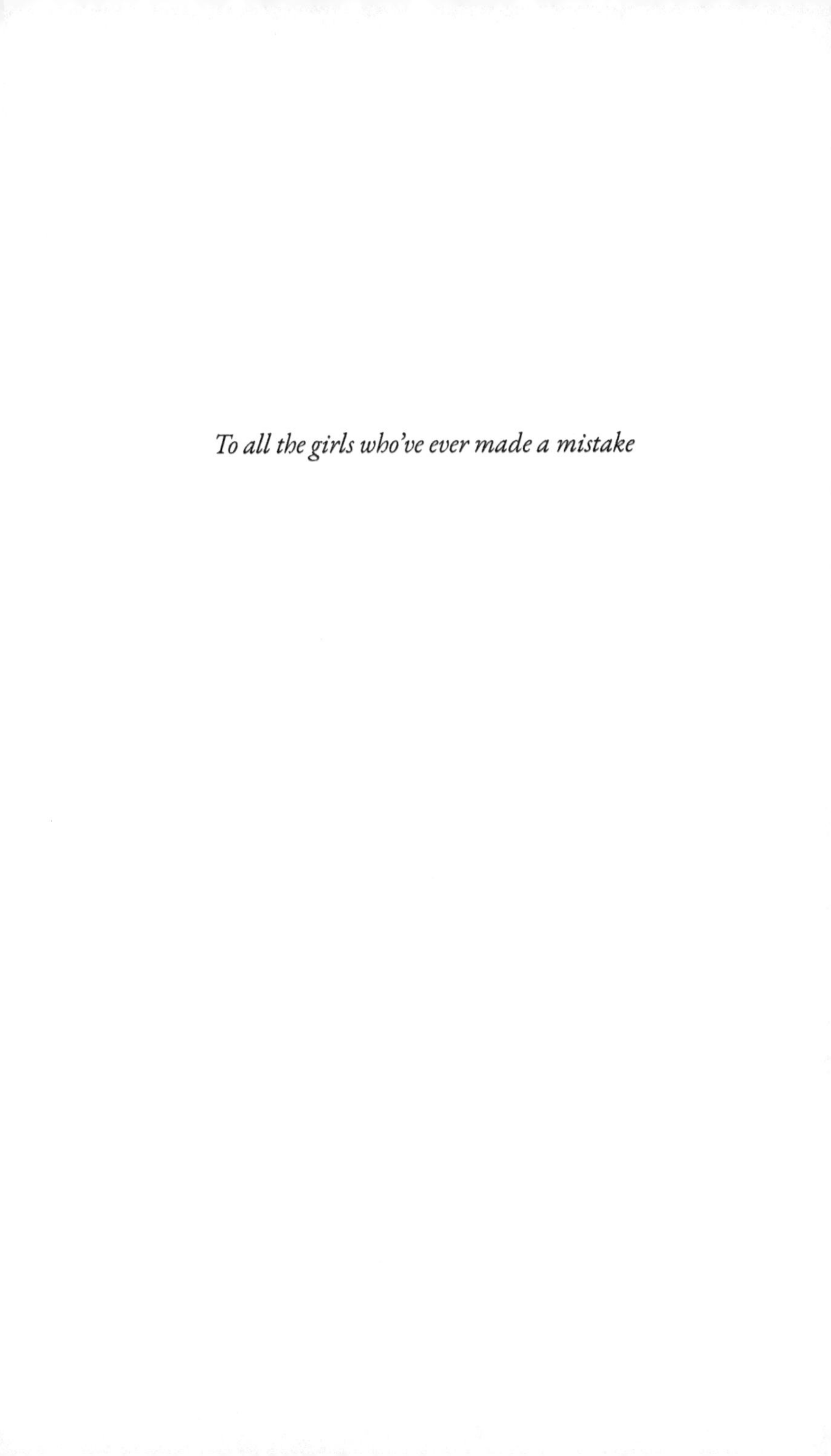

To all the girls who've ever made a mistake

ONE

ALICE

VANE MADDRED, UNOFFICIAL PRINCE OF THE Umbrage, is fucking me like he wants to bruise me.

I'm sure he does.

I clutch at him like he's an oak plank in a churning sea.

We never fuck like we like each other.

Our movements are frenzied, a little punishing.

I think we find ourselves like this most nights because we remind each other of things we hate about ourselves.

He hates that he desires anything, and I hate that I desire one thing I can't have. The fact that that one thing is his uncle is something neither of us will ever speak about.

The floor below us, music thumps against the walls of the Joker's Den.

Sweat coats our skin.

It's the heart of summer and it's always worse in the city where the nearby factories permeate the air with heat and the smell of burning oil.

It's after midnight. I'm drunk but not drunk enough to like myself.

I'm pressed against the wall, my boot braced on the arm of the nearest wingback chair.

Vane is a near carbon copy of his uncle. He towers over me by half a foot, his shoulders broad and muscular. His eyes are violet and bright, his hair dark and unkempt.

But where his uncle is a cliff edge crumbling beneath me, Vane is solid ground, even if it is unforgiving.

"Trying to fuck crown princes now, are you?" Vane asks.

"Yes," I tell him because I know it'll piss him off and I know he'll take it out on me and I just want to feel something, even if it's a punishment.

He growls into me, fucks me harder, his left arm hooked beneath my thigh, spreading me open. His right hand is buried in my hair, fingers like claws, yanking my head back to expose my neck for him.

The hour is here. He and I don't need his clock to know he will be drinking my blood.

Because Vane Maddred is a jabberwocky and jabberwockies need to drink to keep the monster at bay.

His god is time, the tick-tock of his pocket watch his prayer.

But sometimes I think blood is his salvation.

"And were you planning to tell me?" he asks.

"I'm telling you now."

His mouth hovers over my throat.

The "fucker" in question is the Crowned Prince of Darkland, His Royal Highness Evren Lorne. The *official* prince.

We hate him.

Maybe more than we hate each other.

But crowned princes do not make good enemies.

"I'm going to kill him," Vane says and presses his mouth to the rapid thump of my heart in my throat.

"No, you're not." His teeth graze my flesh, and I hiss out.

I'm pent up. Ready to sail. He hasn't given me this much attention in days. Did I bait him by flirting with the Crowned Prince? Yes. Do I regret it? Abso-fucking-lutely not.

Vane is possessive of his toys, and I am his favorite one, even if he likes to break me again and again.

He licks his way up the sensitive line of my throat, and I shiver beneath him.

Maybe I don't hate him.

Maybe he's just enough like his uncle that it quiets that incessant gnawing in my gut.

All of the Maddred men are dark and dangerous and monstrous.

And dark, monstrous things like to be in the company of other dark, monstrous things.

I think that's why we're terrified of losing each other, why we cling to one another, not with love, but the opposite: obsession.

Friction builds between us.

I'm hot and warm and cold all over and when Vane's teeth tickle my neck, I jolt away from him.

"Hold still," he says, yanks my head back, and sinks his teeth into me.

The first hot gush of blood surges out of the puncture wounds.

My veins fill with honey.

Getting bitten by a jabberwocky feels like your bones melt into stars.

I exhale.

To my ears, it sounds like a breath that lasts a lifetime.

I sink down the wall.

Vane adjusts his weight so he can catch me.

Our frenzied fucking slows and the slow drag of his cock is the most sublime feeling in the world.

I'm a puddle, no shape, no weight. I exist only to contain him.

My flesh is sticky in the summer heat, but it's too late to pull off my shirt.

I couldn't move if I wanted to.

Vane drinks from my neck, fills me up and I sway in his arms.

I can feel him growing harder, throbbing against my inner walls. He's described drinking as sexually charged, but if I'm to believe him, I'm the only one he drinks and fucks.

"It's messy," he's said. "And I don't like the clean-up."

Because I know Vane well, I knew he wasn't talking about the *bloody* mess. He was talking about the feelings, the emotional charge, the wake of women he's left trailing after him.

There are a thousand or more on Darkland who would kill to be where I am. A thousand more who would kill me to take my place.

Sometimes, knowing I get all of him, the monster and the man, is more pleasure than an orgasm.

All three of us, Roc, Vane and I, we fuck who we want, but somehow, we always find ourselves here, fucking each other.

"I hate you," I whisper into his ear. But the words come out sounding desperate. Like a wish that will never come true.

He drives in deeper, deeper, harder, harder, as if he cannot get enough of me.

When I first left Wonderland and found myself in Darkland, I thought I would never find a place to set down roots. I'd just lost my family home, and worse, been driven from my world.

But it was with the Madd brothers that I found something new and yet deeply familiar.

And now I want to build something with them, by their side.

Vane drinks from my veins, grunts into me, muscle dimpling in his back, his arms tensing up as he comes.

There is nothing I love more than a Madd brother coming inside of me. As if I'm marked by them, claimed by them.

As if to say, she is mine and she belongs here.

When Vane pulls away, my lifeblood drips from his mouth.

His eyes are glowing yellow in the semi-darkness of our apartment.

"I hate you too," he says and then he throws me into the chair, kicks my legs open, and sinks his mouth to my center.

I arch against the chair, hand hooked over the back, bracing myself.

I'm already soaked, but the blood makes it messier, wet and slippery, and I'm driven to the edge in a flash.

"Fuck," I breathe out. "Fucking hell."

I run my fingers back through his dark hair and grip tightly, driving his mouth into my pussy.

He groans, the sound humming against my clit.

I'm over the edge in an instant, bucking against his mouth.

He hooks his hands around my legs, holding me in place as he eats my pleasure, every last fucking drop.

My breath stutters up my throat as I twitch through the last of the orgasm.

Vane stands up and drags the back of his hand over his mouth.

Blood smears across his face.

His hair is a mess, several strands sticking straight up from my assault.

He's so fucking hot it makes my molars ache.

I want to trap *him* in amber, never let him go.

"Stop fucking baiting me," he says.

We've arrived at the place we both knew we were headed.

"Why? When you make it so easy."

He leans forward, caging me in the chair.

His strong hand comes up, grabbing me by the throat, squeezing.

"Do as I say, Alice. You won't like me when I'm mad." He plants a chaste kiss on the corner of my mouth, leaving a sticky mess of blood, spit, cum, and my juices.

Then he lets me go, buttons up his pants, and heads down the stairs.

I sink back and squeeze the arms of the chair until my nails ache.

Two

VANE

I ENTER THE JOKER'S DEN FROM OUR PRIVATE DOOR in back. It spills in between the bar and the billiards room where walls made of bubbled glass show silhouettes moving around the tables mid-game. Tonight's guest musicians are playing violin and lute along with our piano player, Big John and his son, Little Tom who beats at a handheld drum.

Roc is at the end of the bar waiting for a round of shots to be poured.

"Do you feel better?" he asks and turns to me, his back pressed against the bar, his elbows resting on the nicked and worn dark oak top.

I steal one of the shots before the bartender finishes his pour. "Yes," I answer and sling the drink back. Darkland whisky is smoky and sweet but so fucking smooth.

"You do know she does that just to get your attention."

I'm not about to admit to my older brother that for some fucking reason, I like it when Alice provokes me. It's a game we play on an endless loop. I pretend she doesn't matter and then she baits me and makes me prove that she does.

I come to stand beside Roc and lean into the bar top, sliding the empty shot glass back to the bartender. "Of course I do."

"One of these days it's going to get us in trouble."

"What, exactly, are you getting at?"

Roc angles toward me. "The way you two obsess over one another." He clicks his tongue. "It's not healthy."

"Don't lecture me on what's healthy. You're fucking half the Umbrage."

"Are you slut shaming me?"

"Oh please."

The corner of his mouth lifts. "So, I fuck half the Umbrage...do you see Alice trying to get back at me for it? Flirting with others in front of me? No, because, *one*, she knows I wouldn't care, and *two*, she and I do not obsess over one another. We have a healthy relationship."

"*Healthy*. That's like calling a burger with lettuce a salad."

"I mean..."

"Shut up. Okay, then, what's your sage advice?"

"I wish I had some. I'm just perfect. What I am cannot be replicated."

"Such a fucking asshole."

He sobers, leans into me and lowers his voice. "I'm serious, though. Just figure it out. We have bigger problems to worry about." He straightens, slaps me on the back and says, "Now help me carry these shots to the table."

"You know we have servers for this shit."

"Yes, but they're busy making us money so shut the fuck up and help me."

With a grumble, I grab three glasses and follow him to our table in the far corner.

The table is a half-circle with a booth and three more

chairs positioned in front of it. All of the seats are taken. They usually are.

"Get the fuck up." Roc nods at the man at the end. The man was moving before Roc even opened his mouth, scurrying out of the way to make room for us.

Roc slides in first and I follow behind. Shots are divvied up. There's Comor, our most trusted leftenant; his girlfriend Pen; two of our bonebreakers, Tin and Pike; our cousin, Hana, still a respected member of the Lorne Court; and Callista, a Lorne Court healer, previously a Heart Court blood witch from Wonderland. But we don't talk about that. All of us refugees from Wonderland don't talk about who we were before or what we could do. Calli was one of the most powerful blood witches in Wonderland. Roc and I have tried to poach her from the royal family but she won't budge even though I think healing is beneath her.

Tin and Pike, sitting in the chairs opposite the booth, scoop up the shots before anyone can even suggest a toast. The alcohol is quickly sliding down their throats. They're already drunk. It's their night off so I suppose they're allowed to get fucking blitzed.

"Where were you?" Hana asks, claiming her shot with two tattooed fingers.

"He was falling for the oldest trick in the book." Callista winks at me as she tosses back her shot.

"Christ. Not you too."

Roc drapes his arm over my shoulders and reels me into his side. He smells like cigarettes and blood and liquor. There's a looseness about him tonight, like some of the pent-up energy of the last few weeks has finally abated. He's been a fucking prick the last month as we worked on striking a deal with the Lorne Court to take over Caligo Port, arguably the most important harbor in all of Darkland.

Today we shook hands on it.

Not without a price, though.

"Oh, don't feel bad," Callista goes on, spinning the empty shot glass on the table. Her dark hair is half tied back, with several small braids hanging along her face. There's a silver hoop in her eyebrow and two hearts through her earlobes. She may have left Wonderland a long time ago, but she still wears her loyalty to the Hearts like a badge.

"Alice is a Spade after all," she says. "They really can't help messing with your mind and pulling you down into the baser human instincts we all try to hide, dismiss, or ignore. You want my advice?"

"I don't."

"You can't trust anything a spade says or does."

"It's not like I'd trust a heart either, Call," I say back. "So, you don't have a lot of room to talk."

Comor whistles. "Damn."

The witch pretends not to be phased. And maybe she isn't. I've never seen Calli get ruffled. She served under the Queen of Hearts and somehow escaped Wonderland during the worst of the war. I don't enjoy her company, but I do admire her tenacity.

I've known Alice longer than I've known Callista, but Call has a point. Wonderland Spades are smart, strategic, and sometimes diabolical. It's why Roc and I brought Alice in under our wing. She's good at what she does, gathering info, charming people, bending people to her will.

But sometimes I fall victim to it too. I fucking know that. I'm just not going to admit it to a heart witch.

"Oh look," Call says, changing the subject, "you're being summoned."

I follow her line of sight across the Joker's Den, where a group of people has entered from the inky darkness outside.

Half of the Lorne Court, with Prince Claude and Princess Rosalind at the front, followed by two of the lesser nobles, and

Lady Genevieve beside them. Lady Gen is the daughter of the Duke of Darkland.

It's Gen waving me over.

My shoulders tense up.

"Go," Roc urges me, his expression now serious.

This is the price we had to pay, my duty to our future, compensation for our past.

At one time, Roc was in line to inherit the title of Duke of Darkland. We grew up among the Darkland elite, just as much a part of the Lorne Court as Hana. And then our father tried to overthrow the royal family.

We had anything we wanted. But apparently, everything wasn't enough for Aaric Soren Maddred.

When his plans were uncovered, we went from titled noble assholes to banished assholes, stripped of our titles, our wealth, anything resembling an asset or luxury.

The Umbrage was the only place that took us in.

We were monsters, after all, and monsters make great bonebreakers. Those in power in the Umbrage were happy to use us when they needed people to disappear. Roc quickly became known as the Devourer of Men. He's nearly reached boogeyman status at this point. So, is it a surprise we are now in control of most of the Umbrage? Devouring an asshole or two was worth it.

But somehow, we've circled back to the Darkland elite.

And now they're summoning me to their side.

I don't love this arrangement, but there's no room to have feelings about it.

I will do what needs to be done. And I will do it quietly.

I steal Hana's shot and pound it back.

"Hey!" She lifts her hand in exasperation. "I was just going to drink that."

"Roc will get you a new one."

"I will, Hanny. Promise."

She rolls her eyes at the childhood nickname but gives him a nod.

Gen waves again, more insistently this time, so I slip from the table and make my way across the bar to the future that awaits me.

Three

Alice

Once I'm alone, I collapse into the wingback chair. The crushed velvet smells faintly of Vane, like clove oil and burning tobacco and whisky.

I stretch over the arm, reaching for my cigarettes on the nearest end table, dropped near a stack of Vane's books and one of Roc's trinkets from their past life among the Darkland elite.

I light a cigarette, exhale. Smoke ribbons in the rays of moonlight spilling in through the five large windows at the front of the apartment I share with the Madd brothers.

I've been here nearly four years now. It's as much my home as Wonderland was, but somehow I still feel like a guest. Vane and Roc owned the building long before I arrived, but if I were looking for apartments, this is the kind I would have immediately fallen in love with.

The building itself is a Noir Revival style, with three floors, each one stretching high with twelve-foot ceilings and tall, arched windows. Decorative brackets hold up the roof, and while you'd have to be on the third floor to notice the detail, each bracket is hand-carved with skulls, the jaws yawning open as if they're screaming.

The windows are my favorite. Iron muntins between each delicate pane of glass make a grid on the lower half, while the iron in the arched upper half forms a pattern much like the sun's rays. It's a contrast I love, the symbolism of it all, both light and dark.

The windows overlook Butcher's Row, named as such because it was once the only place to buy meat on the southern end of Darkland.

As the city grew, and townhomes and merchant shops gobbled up cattle lands, the butchers moved further north along with the ranchers. But the name remains. And honestly, what better name than Butcher's Row in a part of town known for making people bleed?

My first night in the Umbrage, I was robbed by a nine-year-old boy with a switchblade and hungry eyes. He left a cut on my arm, my pockets empty, and my ego bruised.

I never made that mistake again.

I take another hit, head lulled back, and close my eyes.

The spirits are loud tonight.

Like a dozen church bells all ringing a different tune.

It's a full moon, the kind that in Wonderland would have been called a Heart Moon because of its red hue.

The dead are always louder on a full moon.

It might be part of the reason why I provoked Vane. Distraction is always better than the alternative.

"She wonders why I left..."

"He murdered me!"

"Tell him I love him."

The different voices wend in and around each other like wind through a forest.

They always have unfinished business. But don't we all?

Over the years, I've gotten much better at putting up boundaries between me and the dead, but in the Seven Isles, I can't see them. I can only hear them, unlike in Wonderland where spirits roam the city streets and the countryside hills endlessly searching for something they cannot touch and sometimes cannot name.

I didn't realize how much of a distraction they were until I left Wonderland. The Seven Isles is like a vacation compared to my home world.

I don't ever want to go back.

And yet, on a full moon, when the voices rise to a cacophony, I am reminded of the strain. My head pounds and my eyes feel swollen even though I haven't cried in months.

Reaching over to the couch where I tossed my jacket, I grab it and yank it onto my lap. Tucked into the inner pocket is an eight-piece newsboy cap constructed of gray tweed.

It was custom-made for me by the Madd Hatter himself, and imbued with a unique power, a fact that I've told no one, not even Vane and Roc.

I slip the hat on, and immediately my body blips out of sight right along with the cigarette.

I don't know why the Madd Hatter made me a hat that turns the wearer invisible. Did he know that some days I can't bear the thought of being perceived? That some days I don't want to exist?

I never asked him, and he never told me.

But it was the perfect gift.

Because when I disappear, even the spirits stop talking to me.

I can just be as I am, just thought and energy and silence.

With no one to hear them, the spirits soon fade away.

I may not see them haunting the Umbrage, but I can feel them, and so I know the moment I'm alone.

The air is still. The room softer. And the chill in my fingertips is finally gone.

I'm tired and cranky, but I promised my best friend, Jade, that I'd join her for a drink before the night was over.

I come down to the Den with my hair combed and my clothing smoothed over. I don't think I look like I've just been fucked by a Madd brother, but Jade won't care. She knows a lot of the details of my private life, Madd brothers included.

As I cross the main bar room, I purposefully don't scan the crowd looking for Vane. I don't want him getting the idea I care what he's doing even though I do.

I find Jade at our table next to the half-circle booth of the Madd brothers. Out of the corner of my eye, I see the chairs are full, but the booth is only half occupied. Roc laughs at something someone says and the rest of the table joins him.

Vane isn't there. I am always distantly aware of him in the room and I sense him nearby, but I'm not about to scan the Den looking for him like some lonely little puppy.

I join Jade, who is sitting with our friend, Salty, who we would consider one of our best if it wasn't for his choice in work. He's a guard in the royal palace and is making his way up in rank. He wants to either become captain someday or join the ranks of the Shadow Order, Darkland's most elite faction of soldiers. Currently he's a sergeant.

We're all originally from Wonderland—Jade a Diamond, me a Spade, and Salty a Club. It automatically makes us kin, in some way. So, Jade and I love Salty, but we don't necessarily trust him. At least not like we would a *best friend*.

I drop into the chair across from Jade and next to Salty. His long blond hair is left loose around his shoulders, with several strands hanging along his face. When I first met him years ago, his hair was buzzed. I think that might have been his last haircut.

He's wearing a plain black t-shirt and black tactical pants. The shirt is loose around his chest, but tight on his biceps.

I didn't know Salty when we were in Wonderland, and sometimes I wonder if I had, if my story would have turned out differently. He's easy to be around, easy to talk to, and extremely good-looking. In Wonderland, Clubs and Spades were allies. It wouldn't have been out of the question for someone like me to find themselves betrothed to someone like Salty. Not that he's ever confirmed his rank or title in Wonderland. I knew *most* of the nobles of the Club court and I don't remember him, but he has a court card, which means he was either born to a powerful family or he stole it from one. Either option says something about him.

In Wonderland, only those with power, status, or wealth possess court cards—magical cards with unique powers that also act as keys to travel through the looking glass. Though you can only travel if you have a wild card, or a full court—a queen of diamonds, hearts, clubs, and spades.

Salty possessing a court card is about the only thing I know about his Wonderland history. Most of us displaced by the Suit War don't discuss our lives in Wonderland. We don't talk about what we left or what we had to do to get here. But most know of the Spade family. It's hard to escape what my parents did and what it got us.

Thankfully, Jade and Salty have judged me on my own and not on the actions and reputations of my family.

"Took you long enough," Jade says and slides a glass to me. It's one of the highball glasses rimmed in sugar, with a bright red drink inside and two slices of orange floating among the ice.

"A Joker Sunrise?" I ask.

"Of course," she answers.

"You know me so well."

I take a sip. The sugar hits me first, then the citrusy, sweet of the cocktail mix, then the heat of the rum. Joker Sunrises make me instantly happier. Jade is truly the best of best friends. From the moment I met her, I felt at ease. There's something practical and sturdy about her. If you're wrong, she will tell you so, but in a very straightforward way. If you're right, she'll clap you on the back and if you're down, she'll find a way to bring you up. Everything about her is honest. You always know where you stand with her.

As long as I've known her, she's worked as the right-hand woman to Warren Ashmoth, the wealthy importer and exporter who owns South Sea Conveyance. They're secretly hooking up. Have been for over a year. The only part about her life she's not forthcoming about. Warren wants to make it official. Jade is still unsure if it's serious, even though he sends her a dozen roses every single Sunday morning, and every time he walks in the room, her eyes light up.

They are in love. The real kind of love that sinks into your belly and crackles like lightning.

Jade leans into me and several of her braids slide over her shoulder and swing behind her. Two of the braids have wooden beads tied into them, the wood carved with Xs to ward off evil spirits. Jade first settled in Summerland when she crossed over, specifically the southern tip where carvings, in beads or trinkets or doorframes, is a common practice to protect the spirit and the home.

I once asked her if she thought they worked and she told me it didn't matter if they did, that the practice itself gave her comfort.

I've never seen or heard an evil spirit. Most I've encountered are neutral, or as neutral as a mortal spirit can be with their trauma and their fears and their hopes and their worries. So maybe there's something to the extra protection. Maybe

Jade's practice, and the practice of others in the Umbrage, are powerful enough to protect us all.

"Salty was just telling me some interesting info," Jade says, lowering her voice. "Something you'll most definitely want to know."

I raise my brows at Salty across the table. "What kind of info?"

Salty leans in too. The three silver bracelets on his left wrist slide forward, chiming together. He's got a good foot on both of us, so he dominates the space quickly, his black shirt bunching up around his broad shoulders. "Vane and Roc were at the palace today."

I've known they've been working on a deal to take over Caligo and that the deal involved the royal family since the unfortunate, *sudden* passing of the entire Caligo family put control of the harbor into the hands of the palace.

Vane and Roc were not the royal family's first choice. They were stripped of their titles, after all, and are now considered mob bosses—impossible to trust, hard to predict.

"Not necessarily clandestine info," I say, slightly bored.

"No." Salty gets a little closer. "But would you know...the Duke of Darkland was there as well."

I pull back, frowning. "Why would the duke join in negotiations over the control of a harbor? He has no stake in imports and exports. None of his businesses sell goods and—"

High-pitched laughter sounds from the billiards room. The kind that scratches against your eardrums and makes your molars clench.

I know that laughter.

It belongs to the daughter of the Duke, Lady Genevieve.

I twist in my chair and glance over my shoulder. I can just make out Vane's silhouette through the murky glass of the billiards room...with Gen snuggled in close to his side.

My gaze snaps to Roc. He's looking right at me, his mouth set in a grim line.

Jabberwockies have heightened senses, including hearing, and though the Joker's Den is full of conversation, laughter, music and the clatter of glasses, I know he heard our conversation.

I know that he knows that I know what the duke's attendance meant. What's the best way to test loyalty? To intertwine your assets. And sometimes, there is no greater asset than a son or a daughter.

Blood rushes through my ears.

My chair scrapes over the hardwood floor as I shove it back.

Roc is on his feet in a second. "Al," he says, a warning, a command.

But I'm not listening. I'm already racing for the door.

Four

ALICE

I DON'T THINK ABOUT WHICH DIRECTION I'M running when I burst out of the Joker's Den and into the alley behind it, but I end up in Wolbridge Graveyard on the western edge of the Umbrage.

I can't really be surprised.

Death has always been a comfort to me, and because I am quick to anger and quick to run away, I often find myself here looking for solace among the moss-covered granite headstones, the old oak trees, and the dead.

I did, however, forget it was a full moon.

When I come to a stop beside the Wolbridge Family Mausoleum, the voices catch up to me.

There are so many, my head immediately begins to pound.

"Fuck. Fuck off."

There are several winding paths through the graveyard, with three of them leading to entrances. I check my position and decide the nearest entrance is to my left and start heading that way at a brisk pace. But I only manage to take a few steps before a hand, all bones and tattered cloth, is yanking me to the ground.

"Absolutely the fuck not," I tell it and shake it off. "Go back to the Underland. I mean...*fuck*. *Die*, my friend. Tonight is not your night for resurrection."

The hand, protruding from a lump of grass and dirt in front of a weathered headstone, goes limp, then sinks back into the earth.

The Seven Isles doesn't have a collective term for the place the dead go. Not like Wonderland. But the term Underland is seared into my brain and I'm not sure I could call it anything else. It's just that the dead here in the Seven Isles don't always recognize the name, and so the commands go ignored.

I don't really know where the dead of the Seven Isles go when they cross over, and when I've asked them, they've had no name for it. Those of us from Wonderland go to the Underland when we die, regardless of where we are when we stop breathing.

Back on my feet, I hurry along the path, careful not to tread near the graves.

"Al! Not the fucking graveyard!"

Roc's voice filters above the din of the dead.

I stop. Sigh.

"Out of all the places," he says with a grumble.

I turn to him. The shadows of the oak tree stretch across the path behind me.

"Why didn't you tell me?" I shout.

"He was supposed to tell you."

Vane.

He had all the opportunity. We were alone, fucking in our apartment. He could have told me when he cornered me in the living room. He could have told me when he was balls deep inside of me. He could have told me after he made me come in his favorite wingback chair.

But he didn't.

I can guess as to the reasons. There would be at least a dozen.

But none of them matter. He let me figure it out in front of my friends.

"Why?" I ask as Roc gets closer. He's taking a drag on a cigarette, his head bowed forward, the smoke spinning behind him.

If you were to analyze my relationship with each of the Madd brothers, it would be obvious that my relationship with Roc is better. We don't fight, not like Vane and me. He tells me everything I want to know and sometimes the things I don't just to make me laugh. Sometimes he surprises me with flowers or jewelry or a trinket he found in some shop somewhere. He smiles more than Vane. He loves to meander and will do so at midnight through graveyards or at noon through museums. If I drink too much and end up puking in the toilet, he'll gladly hold my hair back and then fetch me aspirin and cold water to wash it down.

The only problem is, Roc will never commit to a relationship, which means I never get all of him. Not like I do with Vane.

When I get all of Vane, even as rare as it is, it's like an ocean wave dragging me under. The way he overwhelms me makes me feel like I am living and dying at the same time.

It's addictive. A high I'm always chasing.

All of that is about to change, though.

Roc comes to a stop a few feet from me. He curls his finger over the cigarette, finishing another drag. The glow of the burning ember highlights his otherworldly beauty in the middle of the graveyard beneath the glowing Heart Moon.

I should want Roc more. If I were a math person like Jade, the numbers would add up perfectly.

When he pulls the cigarette from his mouth, the smoke curls out, then gets sucked back in, down, down into his lungs.

"You should have told me. You know he wasn't going to."

Roc exhales and the smoke plumes into the night. "Maybe you're right."

"It's almost like he wants to humiliate me."

"Don't be so dramatic."

"My friends knew about it before I did! Do you know how horrible it is to find out that way?"

He shrugs. "I don't have friends, so no."

"Roc."

"Al."

"Now who's being dramatic?"

He grins at me. "What if I told you—"

A figure covered in clumps of dirt and draped in holey cotton slams into Roc, swiping him from my line of vision.

"Christ," Roc mutters, now on the ground a good six feet from where he was a moment ago. There's a corpse on top of him. Judging by the style of clothing and the desiccated flesh, the man's been dead at least seventy-five years.

"This is why you don't come to the graveyard when you're in a mood," Roc shouts, fighting off the corpse.

"It wasn't planned."

Roc tosses the man back and he lands in the pathway, legs folded at an odd angle, his head, maybe too heavy for what little muscle he has, hangs forward, bobbing like he's drunk.

"Back to bed," I tell him.

"Unnnngghhhh," he mutters.

"I command you to return to your grave."

He manages to get on his knees and crawls across the two-track, over the mossy grass, then wiggles his way back down the hole he crawled from.

"Come on, Al." Roc dusts off his clothes. "How about we get you out of here. I'll treat you to a chocolate croissant."

"Take me for a walk," I counter.

"Of course."

"To Lainey's?" I add.

I haven't seen her in weeks. They forbade me from visiting her while they worked on the Caligo deal. She's technically hidden away in a safe house and we try not to expose her if we can help it and the Caligo deal had a lot of eyes on us. Now, I realize, for more reasons than one.

"Fine," Roc says.

"Yay!" I lunge at him and wrap my arms around his neck. "Oh gods, you smell like the dead." I quickly back off, nose wrinkled.

"Thanks to you."

I flutter my eyelashes innocently. "You know how my power is on a full moon. I'm just a wee little girl, too powerful for her own good."

"Too bratty for her own good." He straightens his jacket. "But in all seriousness, Alice, darling, keep fucking around, and someone will find out about your power and they'll use you up until there's nothing left just like the Queen of Hearts."

This is the reason why no one knows I can command the dead. Vane and Roc both decided it was in my best interest to keep that part a secret so no one in the Lorne Court would take advantage of me. In Wonderland, Spades are known to have a connection to the Underland, but my power is unique. Not even my parents could command the dead.

Though "command" is a bit of a stretch. I don't use the power, so it tends to get away from me when the veil between the living and the dead stretches too thin.

But there are things even Vane and Roc don't know. They think the Underland is an abstract idea, more myth than reality. They don't know that when I was ten years old, I accidentally found myself wandering the Underland, and that it was as real as the earth I walk on now.

FIVE

ROC

PASTRIES ARE NOT MY FAVORITE. I MUCH PREFER peanuts and bourbon and blood.

But a promise is a promise. I am a man of my word, after all.

As we walk, Alice and I share a cigarette. We are silent, but the city is not. Darkland never sleeps. In the distance, I can hear the dockhands shouting to one another. A few dogs bark in a chorus, fighting for scraps. Behind us is the loud rumbling thump and grind of the factories. In front of us, the melody of music grows in volume as we near Fortune's Lane.

Fortune is known for three things: street musicians, good luck trinkets of any shape and size, and pastries.

It's Al's favorite part of the Umbrage as she loves both music and pastries, and while she doesn't believe in luck, I've caught her buying a rabbit's foot or two from the shops on the Lane.

"What's your pick?" I ask her, because we have at least four bakeries to choose from.

We come up on Fortune from the west on Fourth Avenue, where it splits the Lane in half. If we go right, we'll be in the thick of the music and the fortune vendors. If we go left, still more music but fewer trinkets.

"I want to go to The First-Born Baker." Al takes another hit from the disappearing cigarette and hands it back to me.

"I hate the First-Born Baker."

She makes an O with her lips and exhales smoke. "That's because she won't take your shit. It's my favorite thing about her. Other than her croissants, of course." Al smiles up at me, the flames from the gas lamps sending dancing orange light across her face.

There is something special about Alice's features that doesn't exist here in the Seven Isles. There's a flatness to the bridge of her nose, a roundness to her eyes and an equal roundness to her face. Her ears aren't pointy like most of the fae in the Isles, but they aren't soft either. She is the closest thing I have to Wonderland other than Vane and being with her feels like home in a way that's hard to articulate.

Lainey may be our sister with the same mother and father, but she was born here on Darkland soil, and I think despite our shared DNA, the Isles somehow seeped into her blood, making her more Darkland than Wonderland.

Honestly, I'm glad my baby sister has no connection to our homeland. She is the opposite of me and Vane. If we are a boneyard, she is a meadow. If we are a violent storm, she is a morning of sunshine.

She would hate to know her older brother thinks of her as warm and innocent and bright, but in the dark, unforgiving world of Darkland, being all those things is a victory.

I pull on the cigarette, taking the last hit before dropping it on the cobblestones where it hisses and goes dark in a puddle of water.

We go left.

There's a musician on the street corner playing the lute over a tin can slowly being filled with coinage. I flip him a cut, the coin ringing out against the metal and he moves his body in my direction, the music now aimed at me.

He has a singing voice like wheat grass, a dry rasp that I enjoy, but I don't fuck musicians. I have too big of an ego for that.

Fortune's Lane is one of the oldest streets in Darkland and the cobblestones are uneven, the mud between turned black by the soot and dirt of multiple centuries. Because of that, traffic is lighter so it's mostly pedestrians filling the street with some of the shops and vendor stalls spilling over the curb and into the right of way.

Alice and I skirt a tent selling charmed quills and good luck beads strung on leather and chain.

"A charm for the lady?" the man says, stretching his hand out with a flourish. There's a bronze medallion in the squishy cup of his palm with a triangle etched into the metal.

Triangles, especially triangles with a straight line through the top, are ubiquitous in Darkland. The symbol has multiple meanings, depending on who you're asking, but for the most part, it's meant to be a protection symbol, but sometimes it can also mean change.

"No, thank you," Al says, barely looking at the man.

"Ahh come on, sweet girl! So pretty. So small and delicate! You need protection from the monsters of the Umbrage!"

I step out of the shadows, grab Al and push her behind me, then press forward into the man's personal space letting my eyes bleed to bright yellow.

"She needs no protection from the monsters when she has one in her bed."

"Christ!" The man leaps back. The bronze medallion slips from his grip, clattering to the cobblestones. "I didn't see you there, Mr. Crocodile." He makes the sign of the serpent over his face as a way to ward off evil, the evil being me. "Apologies. Sorry. So Sorry!"

The man disappears into his tent, the medallion forgotten in the street.

"A monster in my bed, huh?" Alice says.

"Not a lie."

"If only I could keep him there."

"Don't start."

"I'm not."

"I will never belong to one bed. You know that."

"Never?" The line of her brow lifts. She's playing with me, laughter trembling on her red lips. She already knows the answer to that question—absolutely not, not ever—but it doesn't stop her from trying, from hoping.

I hook my arm around her and pull her in close. "Who am I to deny others the pleasure of my company?"

She groans.

I yank her even closer and kiss the top of her head.

"But you will get the most of me and that will have to be enough."

"It's not," she mutters, but I pretend I don't hear her and she pretends she didn't say it and we go on with our night.

The First-Born Baker is, as the name implies, a firstborn daughter. I usually perform well with firstborn daughters because they're accustomed to caring for everyone around them, doling out orders, cleaning up messes, and being the one in charge. When it comes to the bedroom, usually they are happy to give up control, if just for a moment, so their brain can rest, so the itch can be scratched.

But Kenny has rebuffed every one of my advances and at

first I thought it was cute, a game we were playing, but she keeps doing it.

When we walk into First Born Baker, she looks past the group of customers at the register and spots me. She doesn't react because she's the consummate professional, but as soon as the customers are finished and filing out the door, she crosses her arms over her chest and slings her hip back, giving her curvy body a serpentine form.

God she's hot. Is she doing that on purpose? If she would just give in, I would have her trembling beneath me in record time.

"Hey." Alice snaps her fingers in front of my face. "Stop gaping at Kenny."

"Sorry." I smile at the First-Born Baker. She smiles back, but it's the smile of a gravedigger who's just patted a grave smooth. "Kenny. Looking lovely as always. Did you change your hair?"

Kenny has a mane of thick, bright red hair. It reminds me of the crimson corral on the reef north of Caligo Port. Tonight, and most nights, she has it pulled back in a high ponytail so that inches and inches of red waves cascade down her back.

"Crocodile," she says. "You haven't been stabbed yet?"

I lean into the counter. It's red forest oak with ancient saw marks still visible at the edges. "Oh Kenny. You know I'm a special boy. Only a special blade will hurt a special boy and I'm the only one with the special blade. Did I tell you I'm special?"

Kenny turns her gaze to Alice. "How do you stomach his ego on a day-to-day basis? Also, can you get me that blade?"

Alice sniffs back a laugh.

"She wouldn't dare. I'm her favorite Madd Brother after all. I'm the only one who buys her pastries."

"That can't be true." Kenny tilts her head, the ponytail swinging. "Tell me he's not your favorite, Al."

"Have you met Vane?" Alice says.

This game we are playing is delightful and cute.

I slide my arm around Al's shoulders and tug her into my side. She brings with her the scent of petrichor and tobacco.

I'm not her favorite, not by a long shot. She would push me over a cliff if it meant having Vane. And she would push me and Vane over a cliff if it meant having our uncle. There's a long line of Madd men she's fucked and loved in her own twisted way.

Maybe there's more of Alice in our veins then there is Wonderland.

"I prefer Vane to this one," Kenny says and then slides her hands into the back pockets of her high-waisted trousers. "At least he's quiet."

Alice's shoulders shake with laughter. She glances up at me. "She has a point. You never shut up. You love the sound of your own voice."

"Now you're just being mean," I say, but I can't hide the amusement on my face.

Kenny rolls her eyes.

Alice wraps her arm around my waist and gives me a reassuring squeeze.

"Do you have any of the chocolate croissants, Kenny?" I ask. "Despite what you may think, we did come here for your baked goods, not your enchanting personality."

Alice digs her fingernails into my side sending a sting of pain through my ribs. A warning to behave myself. Acquiring pastries is the highest priority, and any deviation will not be tolerated.

"Pretty please, Ken?" she adds, pretending she didn't just assault me under the cover of love.

"For you, of course." Kenny slides open the door on her side of the glass case and reaches in with a sheet of parchment paper. She pulls out two croissants.

"Make it three," I amend, and she adds one more to a white paper bag. "For Lainey," I whisper to Alice and she nods against my shoulder.

"Good thinking. Who's buying?"

Vane and I have done well for ourselves since taking over the Umbrage, but even so, Alice is not hurting for money. We don't charge her rent or expenses, which means any money she earns just piles up.

"You."

"I didn't bring any money."

"Then why did you ask?"

"I was just being respectful."

I snort and start counting out coins as she adds chocolate crisps, latticed sweet tarts, several petit fours decorated with edible pansies and one gingerbread man because they're Lainey's favorite.

Kenny hands the bags over and taps in a few buttons on the register. "Ten sterling."

I give her two gold dormunds, or dormies, and tell her to keep the change.

Kenny eyes the gold. "That's too much."

"It's never too much for you, Kenny." I wink at her. She frowns. Alice snorts and pushes me to the door.

With our treats acquired and back on the Lane, Alice and I head north for the Darkland Highlands and my baby sister.

Six

ALICE

WE TAKE A CAB TO NOBLE HILL, THE MID-NORTH OF Darkland where the nobility has estate houses on property that butts up against the Royal Grounds and the Palace. From there, we walk. It takes us another hour to get to the highlands, and another hour after that to reach the Maddred safe house on the northwestern coast of Darkland.

I know Vane and Roc, like me, were born in Wonderland and so their early days were spent in some other house a whole world away. But I can't help but think of the cliffside cottage as the origin place of Vane and Roc even though it was purchased just a handful of years back.

The house just feels like the better parts of them. And maybe that's mostly Lainey, her laughter filling up its rafters, her light painting the walls and glowing beyond the bubbled glass.

The cottage sits back from the road at the end of a long, winding dirt driveway. It's two stories with clapboard siding weathered to a dusky gray. There's a carriage house to the right of the main house, and a garden shed beyond that.

Because Roc and I spent most of the night getting here, the sun is just beginning to rise over our shoulders turning the sky the soft, pale blue of forget-me-nots.

Beyond the cottage, below the cliffside, the ocean churns against the rocks, mist glowing in the first rays of sunlight.

The air tastes of salt and earth and dew.

I love it here.

I wish I could live here. I wish I could be with Lainey every day.

But the brothers would never allow it and even if they did, I would rarely see them. If it came down to choosing between the oceanside cottage or the soot and chaos of the Umbrage with the Madd brothers, I would choose them every time.

Using his key, Roc lets us in through the side door. It enters into a small mud room where the black and white checkered floor begins, continuing on through the kitchen. We knock off some of the dirt from our boots, careful to keep it on the rug at the door.

Lainey doesn't live here alone. She has a guardian in Ms. Ollen and Ms. Ollen would murder us if we got mud on the floors. Literally. Ms. Ollen is a retired assassin. She is as much Lainey's housemaid as she is her bodyguard, but Lainey doesn't know that. She hates the thought of having to be babysat. "I'm a grown-ass woman," I once heard her say to both brothers. "I'm old enough to live my own life."

They relented and told her a housemaid was their compromise and Lainey agreed. The fact the housemaid is also an assassin seems to have never crossed Lainey's mind. But Ms. Ollen, despite her history, is loving and kind. So maybe Lainey is willing to look the other way if the possibility ever dawned on her.

"I'll make coffee," Roc says.

"I'll set out the pastries.

I grab several of the ceramic plates from the rack and set them out on the worktable as Roc strikes a match, lighting the gas stove. As the kettle heats up, he readies the pour-over with a filter and the ground coffee.

As we work, golden light stretches across the kitchen as the sun rises over the treetops.

Upstairs, a floorboard creaks, then a track of footsteps.

A few seconds later, someone comes barreling down the stairs.

Lainey darts into the kitchen and lunges at her brother, wrapping her arms around his neck.

Roc sinks into her, hugging her as if she is the only soul who matters.

Watching the Madd brothers with their little sister is jarring.

In the Umbrage, they are towering figures, ruthless, violent, extremely powerful. In Wonderland, they were the most terrifying of all the monsters.

But here within the walls of the seaside cottage with their little sister, they are just men with soft hearts and gentle hands. Men who are acutely aware of the fragility of the people they love. The ones who are not monsters and so have none of the armor.

If love could fill a room, the seaside cottage would burst at the rafters.

I am envious of Lainey in that. Her brothers would do anything for her and I'm not sure I've ever had something like that. Even my own parents chose power over me.

"Alice!" Lainey says next and wraps me in a hug. Her dark hair puffs around me. I can smell her lavender shampoo and her bedtime oil—spearmint and sage and jasmine.

"Good morning," I say into her hair. "We brought treats."

She pulls back and checks the worktable. "First Born Baker?"

"Of course."

She claps, then kisses me on the cheek, then turns and kisses her brother too. "Thank you. You both will be written into my will."

"Lainey," Roc chides.

The only thing Roc hates more than monogamy is the thought of something bad happening to his sister.

Lainey laughs and scoops up a chocolate crisp. "I will die before you. This is a fact. I'm not a jabberwocky. I don't know why you pretend otherwise." A cookie crumb sticks to the corner of her mouth. "Besides, I will make the best ghost."

"Lainey!" Roc says.

"God. You are a wet blanket, dear brother."

I can't help but laugh.

I get away with a lot when it comes to the brothers, but Lainey could get away with murdering them and they'd give her a peck on the forehead for it.

I find it endearing and hilarious.

The kettle starts to hiss, then rolls into a shrill whistle. Roc pulls it from the stove and slowly pours over the ground coffee.

"What are you two doing here, anyway?" Lainey slides onto one of the wooden stools on the other side of the worktable. "I thought you weren't coming until the dinner Sunday night." She picks one of the violet pansies from a petit four and spins it between her thumb and index finger.

"Roc made a concession for me," I tell her.

"Why?"

"Because I was in a mood."

"Why?"

The other thing I love about Lainey is how unfiltered she is. She's not afraid to ask anything if her curiosity is piqued.

There is no such thing as decorum or etiquette with her, even though she was raised among the Darkland elite. I can only imagine how much that annoyed her father, who was concerned with reputation more than anything else.

I never had the chance to meet Aaric Maddred, but I've heard my fair share about him.

"Vane is engaged," I answer.

"WHAT?!" She lurches off the stool. The stool teeters on three legs before rattling back to the marble floor. "Vane is engaged?" she says to Roc, whose back is still to us. I can tell by the tense line of his shoulders that he was not planning to tell Lainey yet and that I've ruined their plans.

"Who is he engaged to?" she goes on. "When did it happen? Do we like her? Wait—" She turns back to me. "Are you okay with this? No, you're not, otherwise you wouldn't be in a mood. Roc, what the hell?" She pivots again to Roc. "Why is Vane engaged? Did Vane agree to this? Is this a business deal?"

"No," Roc answers at the same time I say, "Yes."

Roc scowls at me.

"When is the wedding?"

"It hasn't been announced yet," Roc answers.

I didn't get around to asking, but now that Lainey has, my curiosity is piqued.

"Is there a date?"

With the pour over full, Roc sets the kettle back on the stove. He turns to face us, his body pressed into the corner of the kitchen counter, his arms crossed over his chest.

The seaside cottage kitchen is painted a soft shade of ivory with the many windows draped in sheer linen. In the kitchen, Roc looks like a dark cloud sent to dim the light. And his answer only proves it.

"Next month."

"Next month?!" Lainey and I say in unison.

Oh god.

Oh my fucking god.

Pain shoots through my molars before I realize my teeth are clenched.

They're rushing the marriage so they can ram through their deal to acquire Caligo Port.

It is because of business, I don't care what Roc says. Maybe he believes the engagement is in service to the larger plan, but he's just kidding himself. He's auctioning off his brother for property and access.

Taking in a deep breath through my nose, some of the tension fades from my jaw. I glance at Roc. "Vane agreed to that? To be married in a month?"

"Yes."

I hate this. I hate that Vane gave in so easily. I hate that they didn't even involve me in their plans. All this time, I thought we were working on a future together, that I would have my place by their side.

I was so fucking naive.

The old wide plank floors at the far end of the house creak as Ms. Ollen makes her way to the kitchen. When she spots Roc, she ambles over and puts his face in her hands. "Mr. Maddred! I'm so happy to see you!" She kisses his cheek.

"Good morning, Ms. Ollen," he says and kisses her back. "You're looking ravishing today."

She playfully swats at him. "Stop it. You're teasing me." She's wearing a thick terry cloth robe and loose-fitting black pajama pants with silk slippers on her feet. Her hair is tucked away in a silk scarf tied at the back of her head. She's wearing no makeup, but I rarely see Ms. Ollen with anything more than a bit of chapstick on her lips.

Ravishing is a bit of a stretch, but Roc is always happy to flatter.

"You have good timing, Mr. Maddred. I'm having trouble with the boiler. Could you look at it?"

"Of course."

Roc follows her down into the cellar.

Lainey perches herself on the stool again and props her elbows on the worktable, her chin in her hand. She blinks at me.

"What?"

She blinks again.

"Lainey, stop."

She has the same dark hair as her brothers, hers long and wavy. She's pale, unblemished, eyes wide and observant.

While she has all of the markings of a Maddred, and the same arcane beauty as her brothers, she has fought the undercurrent of darkness running through their blood. She dresses in pastels, ties her hair with ribbons, drapes her tables with gingham and her bed in floral quilts.

Everything about her feels like a warm summer day. Being with her brings me joy.

Except for when she's grilling me with nothing more than a look.

I relent. "Yes, I'm mad."

"What did Vane say?"

"He hasn't said anything to me. I had to hear it from my friends."

Lainey's mouth drops open. "That asshole."

I grab one of the chocolate croissants and take the stool beside her. "I know. I agree."

"You do know the easiest way to get his attention, don't you?"

I wrinkle my nose. "Who says I want his attention?"

"Oh my god. Please."

The aroma of flaky pastry, melted chocolate, and browned

butter hits me. I haven't eaten in hours and hours. "Fine. I'm listening."

I eat as she talks.

"Step one: ignore him. Like seriously, pretend he isn't even there. He will hate it. One time, when we were kids, he refused to play Hearts with me and so I pretended he was invisible for two days and on the third day, he made us a picnic in the garden and played Hearts until my eyes burned."

I admire Lainey's commitment. I'm not sure I have the iron will to ignore Vane. Even when I'm not trying to look at him, I'm drawn to him.

"Step two: make sure he knows you're hooking up with someone else. And not Roc. He won't care about Roc."

I already knew this one. It's why I flirted with the Crown Prince.

"Step three: disappear for a day. Make sure no one knows where you went. He'll lose his fucking mind."

"You might be the most adorable little demon I've ever met. I love you."

She laughs. "I can't take all the credit. I've learned from the best. Uncle Madd is the worst when—"

"Wait." I cut her off.

The laughter dies from her face. "Sorry. I—"

"Was he here?"

"Al . . . "

"Was he?"

She swallows and looks at me and the look says everything.

"How long ago?"

"He left last night."

"He's on the island?"

She shakes her head and my throat constricts.

"He was going to Winterland."

The Madd Hatter was on Darkland, and he didn't come to see me. I should be grateful. I should consider myself lucky.

I can never be sure if Madd is going to fuck me or kill me. He's the worst of the family.

And somehow the only one who makes my palms sweat and my mouth dry.

Terror is a lot like love and I'm not sure which it is I feel for the Madd Hatter. Maybe both.

"Did he stay here?"

The desperation leaking into my voice is pathetic and shrill, but I can't stop myself. I'm like an addict hoping for some everpowder stuffed in a cookie jar.

Lainey nods. "In the blue room."

Every room in the seaside cottage has a color theme and we call the room by its color.

The blue room is on the southwestern corner of the house with wrap-around windows that overlook the vastness of the Seven Isles Ocean.

I lurch away from the kitchen. Lainey lets me go.

I cross through the living room, down the hall. Pass the bathroom and Ms. Ollen's room.

I come up on the last door where it's partly cracked open, all the early morning light spilling in through the windows.

The door creaks on its brass hinges when I push it in.

The bed is made. The candles on the nightstand are out, but are clearly half spent, the cold wax frozen in a drip down the sides.

I can almost hear his breath, the ragged huff of it, the flame guttering and going dark.

The curl of the smoke.

The danger of his touch.

I can smell him here.

Soft leather. Rain-dampened wool. The burn of clove cigarettes.

The press of his lips against my throat, the desire to drink, the inability to do it.

The vibration of power caged behind a curse.

"Alice."

I snap back.

Roc is in the doorway. His shirt sleeves are rolled up to his elbows. A smudge of grease runs over the ink tattooed on his skin.

"You look like you've seen a ghost," he says, quiet, testing.

I'm dizzy and ravenous and restless and angry.

Madd isn't dead, but sometimes I wish he was. Maybe then he'd talk to me.

"I'm just tired," I say and avoid his eyes.

"You want to lie down?" He props his elbow above him on the doorjamb and leans in. "You can stay as long as you like."

There is nothing I want more than to curl into that bed, wrap myself in the thin cotton that Madd used just last night. Sink into the smell and feel of him.

It would be as close as I've gotten to him in years.

"No," I answer and step away. "Let's get back home before it gets too late in the day."

I go to move past him, but he snatches me by the arm and tugs me into him.

His expression is serious, his jaw clenching. "All three of us will break you if you let us."

It's the most honest thing he's ever said to me.

I lick my lips. Nod.

All three of them, the Madd men.

I should run.

I should leave them all behind and find my own way. Make my own life on some other island, with some other man, one who doesn't drink my blood or threaten to kill me or fuck me until I can't see straight and disappear before the day dawns.

A man who smiles at me in a sun-drenched kitchen while he makes me pancakes and pours me coffee.

But even if that man existed, even if he could love me, I would never be the woman who sits, content, in a sun-drenched kitchen waiting for pancakes and coffee.

Not while the dead whispered in her ears.

I've always been drawn to morally grey men because in the gray, I don't have to be so afraid of my own shadows.

"I can handle whatever comes my way, Roc," I answer.

"Yes, but why, when you don't have to?"

He's giving me the easiest out. The chance to leave them, no questions asked.

But how can I? How could I ever exorcise the Madd men from my life?

They are with me as much as the spirits in the ether.

No matter how far I run, I will never escape.

And maybe, deep down, I don't want to.

SEVEN

Roc

ON OUR WAY OUT OF THE HIGHLANDS, ALICE STOPS at a shop and makes me purchase a bottle of Apple Six, a sweet, smooth fae liquor worth twice as much as my boots.

"Is this a cry for help?" I ask her as the road curves out of the seaside town.

"No," she answers and tears off the gold wrapping, shoving it in the pocket of her jacket. "I was thirsty."

To the east, dark, thick clouds build in the sky. I think we might get caught in a storm, but Alice seems in no rush.

"For liquor? At eight in the morning?"

With the cap unscrewed, she hefts up the bottle to her mouth and takes a long drink.

While I was working on the boiler, Ms. Ollen told me we'd just missed my uncle. Even if Lainey hadn't told Alice, I think Al would have figured it out. She has a preternatural ability to sense Uncle Madd as if his presence is a film that's collected on the walls.

When pressed, she's expertly dodged my questions about

their relationship. Vane and I left Wonderland before Alice, before our uncle. Whatever went on between them happened once we were gone, while the war raged. When Alice came through the glass, she was alone, her entire family dead.

"He's never coming back," I tell her. "Not in the way you want."

She takes another long pull from the bottle.

The rolling hills of the highlands spills into the lower lands of the forest where red oak and black pine and alder trees crowd the dirt road.

Thunder rumbles in the distance and the first spit of rain hits my coat.

"Give it here," I say and waggle my fingers at her.

She eyes me, reading my face for my intent, before handing the bottle over.

I take a drink. Apple Six is a bit too sweet for my tastes, but the alcohol warms my insides.

Several more raindrops patter against my coat.

"Where is my place?" she asks, her gaze directed straight ahead.

"What do you mean?"

"With you. With Vane. With all of it." She turns to me, nabs the bottle back. "Do I even belong with you?"

I would argue that she belongs in Wonderland, no matter what we left behind. I knew Al on the other side, so I can confidently say she's different over here in the Seven Isles. Like a sailor who's spent too much time on land, his gaze always fixed on the horizon.

One only needs to spend an hour with her to know there is a constant hum of yearning surrounding her, a hunger that never quite seems satiated. And I know a thing or two about hunger.

"Is that really what you want?"

"What do you mean? Yes?"

"You're still asking questions instead of giving answers."

She huffs out in frustration. "Then I demand a place by your side." She comes to a stop in the middle of the desolate road as lightning flashes in the dark sky above. "With Vane occupied, you'll need someone you can trust."

I narrow my eyes at her. "Can I trust you?"

"What do you mean? Of course you can."

Rain is falling harder now, flattening her hair against her face.

"You're impatient, reckless, extremely possessive—"

"I am not."

"—and you have no control over your power."

"I can learn to be patient."

"Can you?"

"Yes!"

Thunder cracks in the sky, and a sudden downpour opens up.

"Come on." I grab her by the hand and jog ahead to the park that runs through the forest and back toward the sea. There's a garden in the very center with a boxwood maze, a covered gazebo in the middle.

We're soaked by the time we make it beneath the roof. I pull off my coat and shake it out, then hang it over the covered railing. Al does the same.

The storm has blown in warmer air from Summerland, turning the morning humid.

Al runs her hand through her hair, pushing out some of the rain.

"Why are you afraid to return to Wonderland?"

Her hand goes still.

"I can't help but feel like you're looking for something here that you will never find and deep down you know that."

"I'm not going back."

"Why?"

The next crack of thunder reverberates through the wooden floorboards of the gazebo. Alice takes another drink from the Apple Six and winces when she swallows.

"Let's run home, strip off our wet clothes and fuck until we pass out."

"Al."

She pivots, and as she does, some of the tension leaves her shoulders. "Come on. After the night I've had."

"You're changing the subject."

She hooks her arm around my neck, pressing her body into mine. I don't generally need to be coaxed into bed. Al and I don't play games when it comes to fucking. Not like her and Vane do. But I know she's just trying to distract me, so she won't have to answer the question. And okay, maybe it will work. Maybe she knows that if propositioned, I bend easily.

The rain is a driving force on the roof above us. Getting home now will require more walking and a long cab ride and while I'm already wet, I don't much relish the idea of being soaked. My boots are made from extremely hard-to-acquire leather from Lostland. I couldn't replace them if I tried. So we have time to burn.

I run Al back into the railing. She lets out a surprised little huff of air.

"Why don't we wait for the storm to let up and just fuck right here."

She smiles up at me. She's always happiest when she's getting what she wants.

"Okay."

Hooking my hands around her thighs, I hoist her up onto the railing and wedge myself between her thighs.

EIGHT

ALICE

WHEN I'M WITH VANE, IT'S LIKE CLIMBING TO THE top of a tall oak and then peering out to the ground below, the wind rushing up to steal my breath away. There's something disorienting about it.

When I'm with Roc, it's like the tide rolling in, the water settling into a hundred tide pools.

Being with him is just...easy. I don't have to fight it. I don't have to fight him.

His mouth crashes into mine. I arch my back, pressing into him, running my hands through his dark, damp hair. His tongue drives in, tasting me, tasting the sweetness of the fae liquor and all the desire welling up inside of me.

He knows I'm distracting him and myself, but the fact that he lets me is one of the things I love most about him.

Roc does not push. He does not pull. He just bends where he needs to bend, sometimes to get his way, sometimes to give in to those around him.

Our movements grow more frenzied, and when Roc pushes forward again, I can feel the hardness between his legs.

Lightning flashes in the sky again and the electric snap of it seems to echo the thrill in my gut, sinking lower and lower to my cunt.

I don't want to think about Vane. Or Madd. Or Wonderland. Or any of the other things that make me want to scream into the night.

If I have no place, at least I have this, the feel of Roc's hands on my skin, the heat between my legs, the desire throbbing between his.

I groan into him, and the sound seems to spur something in him, because he yanks off my shirt, then unclips my bra and sinks his mouth to my breast.

A hiss of pleasure escapes me as the heat of his tongue drives away the sudden chill of the air.

Still perched on the railing, I arch my back, chasing the comfort of his attention. He grazes his teeth against my nipple, sending a slant of pain and pleasure running through my skin.

"I love the way you taste," he murmurs into me. "I love everything about you. Especially when you're being a brat."

When Roc says it, even though I know he is skilled at flattering everyone, I believe him. Because in these moments, I know he believes it too.

I reach between us, unlatching his belt, snapping it open. He rocks his hips forward making it easy for me.

I unbutton his pants, unzip, and free him quickly.

His cock bobs in the heat, hard and swollen, and when I take him in my hand, he groans into my throat.

"Fuck. This was an excellent idea."

I stroke him slowly and his eyes slip closed, his breath huffing out.

Keeping me balanced on the railing with a hand at the

small of my back, he drops his other to my thigh, his thumb rubbing toward my center.

"Don't make me wait," I tell him, stroking him harder.

His thumb dips, grazing my center and a jolt of pleasure zings through me.

"Get these pants off," he orders, and I hop off the railing so I can shimmy out of them with his help.

We're impatient, frenzied, and he hoists me back up, yanking my panties aside to expose my soaking wet pussy.

He nestles himself into me as he kisses up my throat, licking at my pulse point. The sensation tickles, and I gasp out, shrinking away, making him laugh against my tender skin.

I wiggle my hips and twine my legs around him, forcing him closer.

But he holds himself back.

"Stop," I whine.

"No," he says.

I wrap my arms around his neck. He nips at my bottom lip and proceeds to kiss me everywhere but on the mouth.

"Roc," I moan.

"Al," he says holding himself hard and throbbing against me.

"Fill me up."

"Ask me nicely."

"Pretty please."

He sinks in another inch and a breath heaves out of me.

"Why torture us both?"

"It's no fun when it's over," he says, pinching my nipple between thumb and forefinger. "You always were too impatient for your own good."

I rock back on the railing, teetering over the edge, forcing him to adjust his weight and his stance. He sinks in further.

He laughs against me again, impressed, but the laugh fades into a throaty growl when I clench around him.

He meets my gaze, his bright green eyes almost white against the light of day.

"Fuck me," I tell him. "Give me this."

His dark brows sink over his eyes. Sympathy etches into the fine lines around his mouth. "As you command it, Alice, darling."

And then he sinks all the way in.

I groan, then inhale sharply as he rocks in and out.

Every time he thrusts forward, his pelvis hits my clit, stoking the flame at my center.

I tighten my grip on him. He fucks me harder, faster.

I adjust just slightly, finding the perfect spot so he hits not only my clit, but that sensitive spot deep inside my cunt. Coming that way is my favorite. It's hard and fast and intense.

"You're so fucking close, aren't you?" he says into my neck.

"Yes." I moan.

He reaches between us and soaks his fingers in my juices, then brings them to his mouth. He sucks my pleasure off the tip of his thumb. "Christ, Al. You taste so fucking good when you're getting railed by me."

I smile up at him, eyes heavy. "Don't fucking stop."

"With pleasure."

He grows harder the faster he fucks me and then we're exploding together, clinging to one another, our moans echoing through the park.

Pleasure blinks through me, making me jolt in Roc's arms.

He rocks me back, holding the back of my head in the palm of his hand.

I breathe out at the stormy sky as lightning flashes.

"For now," he says and kisses me once, then twice, "you belong right here with me."

I straighten in his arms and kiss him back and pretend that a question isn't burning on the tip of my tongue.

How long? I want to ask.

But deep down, I know I don't want the answer.

NINE

VANE

"WAKE UP."

Roc's lying on his stomach, his arms tucked beneath the feather pillow. Alice is half draped over him. They're both naked.

Late afternoon sunlight is pouring in through the windows behind me. I heard them stumble in, drunk and laughing, sometime around eleven this morning. Jade told me Alice ran off last night and that Roc ran after her. When I asked her why, she said, "Maybe you should have told her before she had a chance to hear it from someone else."

She didn't elaborate, but she didn't have to.

Did I feel guilty about it? Slightly. I probably should have told her.

Roc opens his eyes and squints up at me. "What time is it?"

"It's nearly five. We're going to be late."

He inhales and groans into the pillow.

Jabberwockies don't get drunk like mortals do, but that

doesn't mean we don't suffer from hangovers. It all depends on the liquor, how much, and whether or not we mix it with blood. I don't see teeth marks on Alice's neck other than mine, so he must not have drank from her.

"Roc," I say, more insistent this time.

"Fine. I'm up." He hefts himself, rolls to his side and slips from the sheet. He stumbles past me for the bathroom.

When he's gone, I find Al looking at me from beneath the messy tangle of her blond hair.

I know she's pissed. I can practically smell it.

"I was going to tell you," I say.

She hasn't moved. Just keeps staring at me. I swear the air stirs.

"Say something, Al."

She pulls back the sheet, revealing her naked body. There are bruises along her thighs and a few more peppering her hips. It's hard to tell which ones are from me and which ones are from my brother.

She grabs one of Roc's shirts from the chair across the room, shrugs into it and leaves the room.

She doesn't say a fucking thing to me.

The frustration spins in my gut.

"Al," I call and follow her.

Our apartment above the Joker's Den consists of the main living space, the living room open to the kitchen. Our rooms break off from there with Roc's to the left of the front door, then the bathroom, then mine, then Alice's. I gave her the front room with the two giant windows overlooking Butcher's Row because I know she likes a view.

I find her in her room yanking on pants.

"I was going to tell you," I repeat because I need her to fucking say something.

"Yeah, well, you had plenty of time, didn't you?" She turns to me and pulls her hair out of Roc's shirt. "But you didn't.

You let me find out secondhand. You made me look like a fucking idiot." She tries to push past me for the door, but I hook her in the span of my arms and run her back. She hits the window casing.

"You think I want to get married? To Gen of all people?"

"Then why agree to it?"

On the surface, I know what it looks like. It's nothing more than a transactional relationship. It would be easy to say it's good for business, because it is. We're getting Caligo Port out of the deal. We'll control two out of the four ports on Darkland, and arguably the two that are the most important.

But Al will see through it.

She'll see through me.

"I have to make amends for what my father did."

Her gaze travels from my mouth to my eyes. A wrinkle of understanding appears between her brows.

"You don't owe anyone anything."

"They don't trust us. Not after what he did."

When it was discovered that my father was trying to overthrow the Lorne Court, he was immediately arrested. I never got the chance to speak to him, to ask him why. All I have are assumptions and I can only assume it was greed and his obsession with power. But now Roc and I have to clean up his mess if we're to make a life for Lainey.

We were stripped of everything. Titles, assets, properties. We had to start over with nothing and a little sister to take care of.

I won't stop now.

"You think marrying one of their own will change their minds?" Al asks.

"It's a start."

"And what about us?"

Deep down, I know I didn't tell her because of this question. Because I didn't want it to be asked and I sure as hell didn't want to answer it.

I lick my lips. Her gaze sinks to my mouth again.

When I'm not with Al, I feel rational. Logic prevails and I can see the way through. Marrying Gen, establishing ourselves among the nobility again, owning the import and export business, it all makes perfect sense. But it only makes sense if Al isn't there.

We are all wrong for each other. We both know that.

And yet we always find ourselves here.

We are like the fable, *Mersa and the Dark Waters*, swimming down and down and down, lungs burning, the bottom always just out of our reach.

And yet we can't stop swimming. We can't help but go deeper. The burn is the punishment and the punishment is the pleasure.

"We can't do this anymore."

My voice is ragged. She practically flinches at my words even though they are spoken in a whisper.

She yanks her arm out of my grip, teeth clenched.

"Fine," she says. "Now get out of my fucking room."

I step back, aware that she's trembling, and two seconds away from slapping me.

I give her a final nod and leave.

TEN

ALICE

ONCE ROC AND VANE ARE GONE, I PULL OUT MY BAG from my closet and start chucking clothes into it.

How fucking dare he?

Somehow, I think I always knew this was where we were headed. I shouldn't be surprised. Half of Darkland wants one of the Madd Brothers for themselves. I was naive to think I'd get one of them, let alone two.

With my bag full, I cross the living room to the front door.

Daylight is already waning and while the moon is entering its next phase, I can still feel the spirits swirling around the apartment.

"Not today," I mutter to them and slip from the room.

There are technically two ways into our apartment. One through the Joker's Den and the other through the alley in back.

I'm not sure where Vane and Roc were going but I don't want to chance running into them in the Den, so I take the alley.

I know where I'm headed.

Less than a half hour later, I'm knocking on the display window of the First-Born Baker.

Kenny spots me through the glass and frowns once she sees my bag. She comes around the counter and unlocks the door for me. Because she's in the heart of the Umbrage, she keeps late hours and doesn't open until seven.

"Which one was it?" she asks, her words sharp with all the violence of a knife.

"Vane. Both. I don't know."

She lets me in and locks the door behind me.

"Fresh donuts in back," she tells me.

I push through the swinging door and drop my bag in her office off the kitchen.

Kenny's shop is one of the oldest buildings on Fortune's Lane. The ceiling is exposed red oak planks with horizontal beams running across it. The wrought iron oven takes up the entire back wall with a few smaller cooktops to the left and a wall of cooking utensils, cookware, and glassware on open shelves to the right. In the center, running from one end of the room to the other, is a weathered worktable with a marble top and hand-carved corbels holding it up.

On the marble worktop, there are four giant sheet pans with donuts lined up in rows. Sugar-glazed and chocolate-frosted. Sprinkled and berry crumbled. I grab one of the sprinkled donuts with the chocolate frosting and drop into the wooden folding chair in the corner. There's a matching chair across from me, with a small folding table between. On the table is a book with a leather bookmark stuck in the center and a half-drunk cup of black coffee beside it.

I pick up the book with my free hand, careful not to get frosting on it. The cover is an oil painting of a battle scene with the title in gold on the top. *The Battle Between Witches and Kings*, it reads.

Kenny doesn't drink coffee, she much prefers tea. And even if she did, she wouldn't take her coffee black. And she sure as hell wouldn't read a book about war.

"Ken."

"Hmmm?"

She's busy dusting the last row of donuts with sugar sprinkles.

"A little light reading?"

She looks up and eyes the book and starts to answer, but her gaze snaps to the left, to the space just beyond me.

"That would be mine." A hand reaches past me and snatches the book from my grip.

"You could have warned me," I tell Kenny.

"You just got here. Unannounced, I might add."

I huff out in frustration.

Nix is one of the wingless fae, his origins unknown. He grew up on Winterland, trained to become an assassin by the secret society, The Ancient Order of Shadows. He's extremely skilled at casting illusions, one of the best if you ask anyone who knows him.

I met him a few years back when he was passing through Darkland. He stays with Kenny when he's not on an active job, and occasionally he will make an appearance at the Joker's Den to harass Vane and Roc with just his presence.

The brothers don't talk about him much, but I get the distinct impression that Nix is one of the very few men they would never quarrel with if they could help it.

"Hello, Nix," I say.

"Hello, love." He sits across from me, positioning the chair so he has a full view of the entire kitchen, his back against the wall.

"What brings you to Darkland?" I ask.

"Oh, you know. A little of this. A little of that." He smiles at me.

When I first met Nix at the First-Born Baker's shop, he was wearing round, black framed glasses, a white button-up shirt and black trousers. His hands had been shoved in his pants pockets, his broad shoulders slightly stooped as if he was uncomfortable with his tallness, his size, uncomfortable with being in the room. He barely made eye contact with me and spoke in low tones, careful never to raise his voice.

I'd thought he was a librarian or a scholar or something benign.

And then the next morning, one of the councilmembers in the Darkland High Chamber turned up dead and I learned that there is nothing shy, innocent, or benign about Nix. All of it was a mask to hide his true self—that of a competent, efficient killer.

"Are you here to kill someone?" I ask him.

He rests his head back against the wall and looks at me.

His silence is punctuated by a smile.

Living with the Madd brothers, I like to think I've grown immune to the disarming nature of extremely handsome men, but Nix is an exception.

His black hair is on the longer side, but he usually keeps it tied back in a bun. His darker complexion reminds me of a desert at sunrise on a hazy morning. His eyes, too, remind me of the earth, too light to be brown, but too brown to be orange.

He has just one distinguishing mark—one vertical bar tattooed on the inside of his left arm. The mark of the Ancient Order of Shadows. And the mark, when passed beneath a special light, will glow with a wisp of shadow inside of it.

"Who are you here to kill?" I ask him when the silence finally gets to me. "Is it me?"

"If it is, you'll find out soon enough."

"Don't be a dick, Nix," Kenny says as she dusts off her hands, pink sugar glittering as it rains down to the worktable.

I take a bite of my donut. "If you are here to kill me," I say, mouth full, "at least let me finish my treat."

His smile grows larger and a laugh huffs out his nose. "Oh Alice, I could never kill you."

"Now you're just trying to flatter me."

From behind me, I hear the whisper of a spirit.

Death follows him everywhere.

Nix narrows his eyes. "What just happened?"

"Huh?"

"You just checked out." He sits forward, arms folded on the table. "Like you heard something."

Something else I find incredibly hot about Nix is how fucking perceptive he is. Which is also frustratingly annoying. Because I can't hide anything from him when half of who I am is meant to remain hidden. I can't tell him or Kenny that I can talk to spirits or raise the dead.

"I thought I heard someone at the window." I pick at my donut, letting my face fall. "I was hoping...actually, no. Never mind. I'm not going to tell you all of my embarrassing short-comings."

"You were hoping it was a Madd brother," he guesses, and I let him think he's right.

I sigh and rock back against the chair. "Yeah. Vane. It's stupid." I put emphasis on *stupid* like I'm a vapid, dumb girl. Nix will read through it, but he also knows how deeply entwined I am with Vane and how I feel about him. So, it's not necessarily out of the question that I would be acting like a vapid, dumb girl.

"What about Vane?"

"He broke things off with me because he's engaged."

Nix lets out a whistle and sits back. "Brutal."

"I know."

"Who's he engaged to?"

"Lady Genevieve."

"Oh, for fuck's sake," Kenny says. "She's been trying to get him for months. Years. She probably begged Daddy to make it happen."

"You have to admire the work," Nix says. "It's not every day one of the nobility chases one of the Umbrage bosses."

"Vane may have been stripped of all his societal standings, but he's still a Maddred."

"True." Nix takes a drink of his coffee. "And I assume he does not have your blessing?"

"Of course not." I wrinkle my nose and tear off another piece of donut. "Gen doesn't deserve him. I'm the one who's been by their side the last four years."

"So, what do you plan to do about it?"

"I don't know. This is step one of my plan. Hide at Kenny's." I might as well test Lainey's three-step process. I have nothing to lose at this point.

"And step two?" Nix asks.

"Make Vane jealous."

"Spite. Nice."

An idea occurs to me. "You could help me."

He wraps his hand around his coffee mug. "I'm listening."

"Come with me to the Joke's Den. Pretend we're hooking up."

"Oh, darling. When I'm on a job, I don't pretend."

Heat rises up my throat. I glance across the table, meeting his eyes, and with a blink, Kenny's kitchen is gone. We're in a dark bedroom, a king's bed draped in silk sheets. And we're fucking like we're racing death's ticking clock.

I lurch away from the table.

The illusion breaks.

Nix laughs, the sound rumbling in his throat.

"What did you do?" Kenny chides.

"Just showed her the possibilities."

The appeal is hard to deny. There is nothing I want more

than to get beneath Vane's skin the way he always gets beneath mine. And if I get to hook up with Nix in the process? A bonus.

"Are you serious?" I ask.

Nix shrugs. "I have some time to kill."

"How much will it cost me?"

"To antagonize the Madd Brothers? Consider this one on the house."

I don't go home that night.

Instead, I spend it in Nix's bed.

He fucks like he kills. With precision. With skill. His eye always on the objective: to make me come.

I don't feel bad about it. In fact, after my second orgasm, lying next to him in the spare room in Kenny's apartment, I wonder why it took me so long.

"You're really good at this," I tell him, my breathing still labored.

It's somewhere after three in the morning and moonlight is spilling in through the bedroom windows. He expended as much energy as I did and yet he isn't sweating, his breathing even.

"I know," he says, dead serious. There is no underlying tone of ego in his answer. It's just a fact.

"I feel like I should be paying you."

"I don't take money for sex." He turns into me, hooking me around the waist. A second later, I'm straddling his hips, nothing but the sheets between us. His hair is still tied back, but several strands have come loose, trailing down his neck. In the moonlight, he looks every bit the assassin he is, impossible to read, tempting to know, quietly dangerous.

All around me, spirits whisper in my ear.

If I could bat them away, I would.

"Where will you go after this?"

His fingers trail down from my waist over the outside of my thigh. Goosebumps follow his touch.

"I have a job on Lostland."

"Seriously? How do you get there when no one knows the way?"

"I know the way."

The tips of his fingers follow the curve of my thigh, down to the sensitive inner flesh.

"Can I go with you?"

I'm not sure where the question comes from, but it's out before I can stop it.

"You want to go on vacation with an assassin?"

"Why not?"

He grazes the seam between my thigh and my pussy and a hiss escapes me. I'm still sensitive to his touch, adrenaline still thumping through my veins.

"You can't run from your problems."

I roll my eyes and slide off of him, annoyed.

Men are always telling me what I can and cannot do.

"I don't have problems."

Nix shoves me over to my belly and climbs on top of me, covering my body with his. His cock is half hard, pushing between my thighs.

"We all have problems, love."

I don't want to think about my problems. I don't want to think about how the one man I loved the hardest left me to fend for myself. How afterward, I went looking for his replacement and somehow found myself entangled with his nephews, two men who are equally unavailable.

I don't just have problems, I have a nest of poisonous snakes.

Nix rocks his hips and his cock thickens, pressing closer to my center.

I arch my ass up, meeting him.

"For once, I wish someone would let me run," I hear myself saying.

"If you want my advice, the further you run, the quicker your problems catch you."

His hand comes around, fingers wrapping around my throat.

I am distantly aware that he could kill me in a thousand creative ways.

Nix's mouth comes to the soft curve of my ear, his voice confident, sure. "Spread your legs for me."

I wiggle beneath him, opening up more.

He slides in easily. I'm still wet and messy from our last session.

The whisper of spirits increases and a chill rolls down my spine despite the heat of the room and the heat of Nix pressed against me.

He rocks his hips forward, filling me up and I moan out into the pillow as his fingers press harder at my throat.

"Fucking you feels like how I imagine dying is," he answers.

And for some reason, that gets me wetter. Because I know what he means even if he doesn't entirely understand the connection. I've always been a gateway to the other side, the key that neatly fits into the lock of the dead. And who better than an assassin to know what the edge of death feels like? I am as close as he will come to experiencing what he does best.

Or at least that's what I tell myself as he shoves into me.

Someone like Nix, like Roc and Vane, can have anyone they want. And there is power in being the chosen one, if only for a night.

Nix finds the right angle, thrusting inside of me, hitting just the right spot.

The pressure builds quickly like a storm building over open water.

Suddenly I'm coming, loud and high-pitched, and Nix increases his tempo, chasing the pleasure with me.

"I love hearing you moan," he says, his words husky and urgent as his hand clamps over my mouth, "but Kenny will absolutely kick us out."

His hand drowns out any noise and my breath huffs out around his fingers as he sinks in deeper, his own groan huffing into my ear.

"Three loads, two holes, in less than twelve hours." He pulls out slightly, then rocks back in slowly. "They're going to smell me all over you."

The illicit thrill of it dances through my lower abdomen.

He's right. Jabberwockies have heightened senses. And I'd be lying if I hadn't already thought of this.

His hand slips away from my mouth, and I breathe out against the pillow. "Just to be sure, I could take a few more."

He laughs and rolls off of me. "We do have plenty of time for it."

"Challenge accepted."

ELEVEN

VANE FINDS ME ENJOYING MY SECOND ESPRESSO IN the backroom of the Joker's Den.

"She didn't come home last night."

"Good morning to you too."

"Roc, for fuck's sake. Alice didn't come home."

"So?"

"So?" He drops into the matching leather club chair across from me. "Where the fuck did she go?"

"Is it really any of our business?"

He scowls at me, violet eyes glinting. The answer is no, it isn't any of our business, but the look on his face clearly says he thinks it is.

"You're soon to be married," I say.

He grumbles in the base of his throat and yanks out a pack of cigarettes. He lights one as I continue.

"And correct me if I'm wrong, but didn't you tell Alice she and you were done?"

The end of the cigarette flares as he inhales on it, the

smoke curling around his face. When he exhales, the room grows hazy with smoke.

"All of that is beside the point."

"Is it?"

I overheard Lainey schooling Alice on all the ways to deal with Vane. I know that she's likely disappeared as a way to teach him a lesson and while I don't necessarily agree with her tactics, it's clearly working. My brother and Alice have always had a toxic relationship. Like oil and water but the oil is on fire and the water is boiling.

I don't like to tell him what to do—I doubt he'd listen to me anyway—but part of me had hoped this betrothal would end some of the drama.

Apparently, I'm a fucking fool.

Truly I should have known better. My little brother has fucked around with a lot of women in our days, but none he's latched on to like Alice. None he's claimed in any proprietorial way. I think on a subconscious level, he sees the abyss in Alice, and the only place Vane has ever allowed himself to be real is in the dark, a place where no one can see him for what he truly is.

Maybe they aren't so much oil and water as they are a yawning black hole trying to devour one another.

"You have more important things to attend to," I remind him. "We're due to announce your engagement in..." I take out my pocket watch. "...four hours. You should be getting ready instead of harassing me."

He sits forward, elbows on his knees. "You don't know where she is?"

"No. She didn't tell me and I wouldn't have asked anyway."

He takes another long pull on the cigarette while staring at me.

I tsk at him.

He exhales another puff of smoke.

"What? Is there more?" I ask.

"I heard Nix was in town."

Well now he has my attention. And clearly this was where we were headed.

"When?"

"Two days ago."

"He got a job?"

"Don't know."

I snap my pocket watch shut. "Let me deal with this. You stay here and behave."

"What are you going to do?"

"Pull a wild card."

South Sea Conveyance is on the east end of Needles Harbor. Warren owns a quarter of the docks, the warehouse on the harbor, and an office building directly across from it. He built his business from nothing, arriving on Darkland when he was just a teenager. He started as a dockhand and worked his way up. But his holdings truly took off once he hired Jade to manage the financials. I've tried to steal her from him multiple times, but she's loyal to a fault, a quality I admire when it's someone on my side.

I find Jade and Warren in Warren's office in the back. The building is a converted candle factory that still smells faintly of tallow and beeswax. The entire first floor is open, with a loft-style second floor accessible by an open steel staircase. Beneath the loft, Warren's office runs the entire width of the building, with the front-facing walls constructed entirely of grid windows.

"Is this business or pleasure?" Warren asks, rising from his desk to clasp my hand and yank me into a half-hug. Warren is a foot taller than I am, corded in muscle, shoulders broad. His back is always straight, his head always held high. And yet there is an ease about him that makes one feel like they've come home to an old friend.

Despite all that, he is ruthless in business when the situation calls for it. Somehow, he managed to scoop up his quarter of Needle Harbor before I even knew it had come on the market.

"A little of both, I suppose. Though I didn't come here for you."

"Oh?" He lifts a brow and eyes Jade behind me.

I turn to look at her. She's leaned back in her desk chair, arms crossed over her chest.

"Jade, you look lovely today."

She knows me better than that.

"What do you want?"

"Have you seen Alice?"

Her eyes narrow.

"I don't need to know where she is, but if you could get a message to her and please ask her to come home, I would forever be in your debt."

Jade stands up. She shoves several long braids off her shoulder as she comes around the desk and crosses the room to me. She's petite, the top of her head barely reaching the line of my shoulders, but her presence has always been larger than her frame. She doesn't need size to stand toe-to-toe with the men of the Umbrage because she's smarter than 99% of them. Probably me included.

"Is it still her home?" she asks, her gaze carefully scanning my reaction, logging it, analyzing it.

"Yes."

Several lines appear between her brows. "Hmmm."

"Please, Jade."

"Why?"

"Because Vane has Very Important Business to attend to tonight and I don't need him distracted."

"You mean he wants to have his cake and eat it too."

She isn't wrong. See? Smart.

"I will concede the fact that Vane is being an asshole. And I will concede the fact that Alice is technically not gaining anything by returning home. But it will buy me time."

"Until?"

"Until...until...well I don't know. I don't have all the answers."

"You didn't come very prepared."

Behind me, Warren snickers. I shoot him a look and he buries his grin behind his hand.

I inhale. "Even you must know that eventually, Alice needs to go her own way. But tonight isn't the night for it."

"No, Vane just needs a few more nights to fuck her over, leave her a little more broken."

"You know we're all a little broken in the Umbrage."

She considers me for several long beats, and then, "Fine. I'll ask her. But I'm not making any promises."

"No promises needed. Thank you." I turn to leave.

"Roc?" Warren says.

I glance at him from the doorway.

"I hope you know what you're doing."

I smile. The answer is on the tip of my tongue. *Of course I do.* But the words don't want to come out, almost like my tongue knows it's a lie.

TWELVE

ALICE

NIX HAS HIS ARM AROUND ME WHEN WE WALK INTO the front door of the Joker's Den.

Jade found me at Kenny's and gave me the short version of Roc's plea.

Next time I see Lainey, I have to give her a big kiss on the cheek. She was absolutely right about disappearing for a while. The fact I disappeared and ended up in Nix's bed was just a bonus.

When we walk in, attention follows us.

I don't spot Vane and Roc right away, so I cross the room to my table in the back. Jade, Salty and Warren are already there.

"Bold!" Salty says and raises his glass to me.

"Have they announced it yet?" I ask Jade.

"Not yet."

Earlier today, I'd considered forgoing step 2 of the Lainey plan and leaving Nix behind. But when Jade told me Roc wanted me home specifically for Vane's engagement announcement, I dug my heels in.

If he wanted to rub salt in the wound, then I would throw fuel on the fire.

I know none of this is healthy or right, but I don't care.

Sometimes I want the Madd brothers to feel some of the pain they inflict on others.

Salty orders us drinks. The table quickly fills up with Joker Sunrises and tumblers of Summerland whisky. I down my whisky, then immediately turn to my Sunrise. I don't want to feel anything at all tonight. Most of all, depressed.

We're laughing at one of Salty's stories when Vane and Roc come in from the back entrance.

Vane's attention shoots to me, then to Nix close by my side. The moment he sees the assassin, his jaw clenches, teeth grinding hard against each other.

Sometimes, when I'm with Vane, I think of a quote I read years and years ago in a dusty Wonderland library.

All extremes of feeling are allied with madness.

And what's more extreme than obsession?

I'm not even sure why Vane and I play these games, why we're both reluctant to walk away, so desperate to win.

In my brain, I know he's bad for me. Like a glass of milk that's sat out too long, that's curdled and turned sour.

And yet all logic leaves my brain when he's in front of me, when he's pretending I belong to him and no one else. I sink my teeth into him just as much as he sinks his into me. And we are forever gnawing on each other's bones trying to satiate a hunger that can never be turned.

He crosses the room.

All eyes are on him, including mine.

I can never stop looking for him and looking at him.

I should walk away.

I should leave Darkland for good and never look back.

Halfway through the Joker's Den, he snaps his fingers and several of his men fall in line behind him.

The volume of conversation in the Den lowers until their voices are just hushed whispers.

When Vane reaches the table, his leftenant is beside him with three of their Bonebreakers behind them.

"Should I be flattered?" Nix says.

The entire Den is hanging on, waiting for Vane's response.

"Did you miss the sign at the door? No assassins allowed."

"He's here as my guest," I answer, but Vane doesn't look at me. He just stares at Nix.

"I just want to drink and celebrate." Nix winds his arm around my waist and tugs me closer to his side. Vane follows the movement.

My heart is thumping hard against my rib cage.

I don't know why adrenaline is pumping through my veins with the heat and speed of a thrill.

This shouldn't be thrilling. This should be annoying.

And yet...Vane is doing all of the things I wanted him to do. To show that he cares, even though he insinuated he didn't.

"Leave, Nix."

"Or what?"

Vane pulls out his pocket watch and checks the time. "Or I'll let time run out."

Not many people this side of Wonderland know what Vane and Roc are. They've heard the stories, given some weight to the rumors. But the brothers don't shift in broad daylight if they can help it, which means all of the stories have stayed stories.

The fact Vane is threatening to show his cards proves just how much he *does* care.

About me.

Can I stop this marriage? Can I make him mine for the rest of our days?

Is that even what I want?

I'll figure it out later. Right now I have my proof and that's enough.

I pull away from Nix's side and stand up, gesturing for him to follow me. "I'll walk you home."

"No, you won't."

I look over at Vane. "You told him to leave. So, we're going to leave."

"You're not going with him."

"Yes, I am."

Vane pivots his body, angling toward me. "No, you're not."

My heart lodges itself in my throat as anger burns up my sternum.

I am both vindicated and pissed. He doesn't get to marry someone and then dictate every little thing I do on the side.

"It's all right," Nix says, and gets up behind me, his chest to my back. He draws his arm around my waist, sinks his mouth to my neck and kisses me. Vane and I continue to stare each other down. "Come find me when you can," Nix adds and then guides me up to his mouth with his hand on my chin. We kiss and we make it count.

When we pull back, Vane's eyes are glowing yellow.

"Congratulations on your upcoming nuptials," Nix tells Vane. "I'm sure you'll love the life of a husband."

He laughs and pushes out the door.

THIRTEEN

VANE

Roc grabs me by the arm and yanks me out the back door and into the alley that runs behind the Joker's Den.

"What the fuck are you doing?"

I light a cigarette and drop myself onto a small stack of crates, some of the adrenaline ebbing out.

Some of the fog has cleared from my head and the needling feeling of regret pulses behind my eyes.

It was a bit reckless, a bit impulsive, but it wasn't without reason.

"Whether she likes it or not, she belongs to us. And if it belongs to us, it must be defended."

"We claiming women like property now?"

"No." I take another hit trying to orient my thoughts. "It's not about her. It was never about Alice. It's about us."

Roc crosses his arms over his chest. "I'm listening."

"If the Umbrage sees us capitulating to a girl, then to Nix, what then? The whole point of me marrying Gen and negotiating Caligo Port is for fucking power, Roc! We can't grow soft now."

"So, this has nothing to do with your desire to control Al? To have her when you want and only when *you* want."

"No." The word comes out too quickly, tasting sharp like a lie.

My big brother, who knows me better than anyone, can see it too. But none of that matters. Not right now anyway.

"We lost everything at one point. And we could easily lose it again." I look up at Roc. "And then what kind of life would we give Lainey? We owe her something beautiful and safe. Mother and Father couldn't give it to her, not with any kind of permanence. So, it must be us. It has to be her big brothers who build her something lasting."

Roc exhales and leans against the brick wall of the Den, some of the tension leaving his body. "Alice isn't going to let you get away with this so easily."

"I can handle Alice. Let me deal with her and our fucked-up relationship at a later date."

He snorts. "Good luck with that, dear brother."

How much time can I buy myself? A day? A week? I'd prefer a fucking year, but Alice is even more impatient than I am. I'm shocked she isn't out here right now demanding I answer for myself.

One of the crates further down the alley rattles and a dog saunters out. I thought I'd heard another heartbeat nearby. I whistle to him and he ambles over. Some of his ribs stand out against his dark fur. "Hungry, boy?" He looks up at me with heavy eyes.

Roc pulls open the back door and shouts inside for Comor. Our leftenant comes out a second later.

"Feed this mut for us," I order. "And some fresh water too."

"You got it."

I give the dog a scratch behind the ears and he sits back slowly on his hind legs.

"Lainey would love you," I tell him. "She's always begged for a dog."

"When this is all done," Roc says, "let's take a week off and go spend it seaside with our sister. We can take the mut with us. She could use a watchdog. Ms. Ollen may be a retired assassin, but she's closer to courting death than she is to greeting the morning."

The back door opens again and Comor appears with a bowl of leftover steak and another with fresh water.

"Make him comfortable, Comor," Roc says. "We're keeping him."

"Got it."

I straighten. "This vacation, is it before or after I get married?"

Roc shrugs. "I'll leave that up to you. You think your new wife will let you disappear for a week at a time?"

"Let? I don't need anyone's permission."

The dog whines and turns his head, staring down the end of the alley at nothing but the night.

Roc laughs and slaps me on the back. "You're going to make the best husband. I can see it already."

Comor sets the bowl down. "Who, Vane? He's going to be the worst husband ever."

Roc laughs harder.

"You can both fuck off."

FOURTEEN

ALICE

WHEN THE DOG CATCHES MY SCENT, I RACE OUT OF the alley.

I knew eavesdropping on Vane and Roc would only make things worse, but I couldn't help myself. And now I'm glad I did it. Now I know where I stand.

Tearing off the hat, I'm suddenly there again on the sidewalk, with hands and feet and hair and shoulders.

My body settles back into itself.

I shove the hat into the inner pocket of my jackets.

Back inside the Den, the music kicks up around me. We're still an hour away from the announcement and the celebration that follows. But I've already heard enough. I've already seen enough.

I'm not someone who needs to cry often, but right now I feel like sobbing alone in the dark is the only way I won't end up screaming.

I make my way across the main room giving Jade and Salty an apologetic nod as I go. They'll understand. I know they will.

But before I make it to the backroom, I'm cut off by two figures dressed in gold and black.

On the right, is Callista, the Heart Court witch, and on the left, Lady Gen.

That urge to scream grows in the base of my throat.

"What do you want?" The question is pointed at Gen, but it's for the witch too.

"Whatever it is you have going on with Vane," Gen says, "it's done now. He's mine."

I roll my eyes. I don't have time for this dick swinging. Not when I feel like I'm two seconds away from burning this entire place to the ground.

"You can have him." I sidestep her, but she counters me. "What, Gen? What the fuck do you want?"

"It's Lady Gen," the witch corrects, her mouth curving into a smug grin.

I cross my arms over my chest and wait.

"Vane is mine," Gen repeats.

I can't stop the laughter from bubbling up my throat. "You have no fucking clue what you've gotten yourself into."

She curls her upper lip. "You're just a jealous bitch who thought she could climb her way out of the gutter."

"You think you can handle Vane, do you?"

"Of course I can. He'll be my husband. He chose me."

It takes everything I have not to spit laughter in her face.

"Good luck with that. Good luck to both of you. You're going to fucking need it."

Later that night, after the engagement announcement, after the drinks have been drunk, after the moon has set, I come out of my room for a glass of water and spot a pocket watch abandoned on the end table by Vane's favorite wingback chair.

I stand there in the darkness staring at the watch for too long, temptation and anger burning through my veins.

I snatch the watch from the table, pop out the pin, and roll the time back by an hour.

If Gen thinks she can handle Vane, *every part of him*, then she'll have no problem facing him at his worst.

Fifteen

Vane

"What are you thinking about?" Gen asks me. "You seem far away."

If I tell her I'm thinking about Alice, it'll only bring trouble.

Alice hasn't spoken to me since last night when I forbade her from seeing Nix. Not when we all stumbled up to the apartment. Not this morning as she carefully brewed a pot of coffee. Not this afternoon when she came out to grab lunch, then disappeared again into her bedroom, slamming the door behind her.

Now, she's at her table with Jade and Salty and Warren. She's still on her first drink, which is unlike her. When she gets started on Joker Sunrises, she finds it difficult to stop. She's barely drank half her glass.

In the billiards room, Roc is playing a game with the Captain of the Royal Guard, while Princess Rosalind hangs on him, angling for his attention. Now that it's clear the royal family is fine with us Madd brothers re-entering the royal fold,

I wouldn't be surprised if the princess tries to marry Roc. She's always had a thing for him. I think if our father hadn't tried to overthrow the Lorne royal family, Roc would have been forced into a marriage with her anyway. At least now it'd be his choice.

"Are you nervous about our upcoming wedding?" Gen asks.

I should pretend that I am. It would explain my aloofness, my inability to give her any attention. She's meant to be my wife. I'm meant to bend her over and fuck her until she screams my name. But I can barely summon enough energy to look at her, let alone get hard for her.

"Why would I be nervous?" The question comes out sounding bored and distant.

Gen frowns at me. "Then why are you distracted?"

Alice laughs at something Salty says. Salty is angled toward her. He can't stop smiling at her.

Are they fucking too? Salty has always had a thing for her.

Take a breath. Calm the fuck down.

I inhale through my nose, fill up my lungs. Count to four.

Alice doesn't matter. I gain nothing with her. Only trouble.

"I just have a lot on my mind," I say to Gen, hoping that's enough to assuage her incessant worrying.

"Like what?"

Christ.

"Business."

She frowns at me.

I take another breath and then slide in closer to her on the bench seat. She leans her body into mine, puts her hand on my thigh.

I can't believe I'm marrying this girl in less than a month.

I have to constantly remind myself of the duty to our business and our family. That it's for the greater good. But it feels like a big fucking mistake. A huge fucking inconvenience.

I'm shit at being a boyfriend. What the fuck do I know about being a husband?

"Why don't we go upstairs to your room?" Gen asks and slides her hand further up my thigh.

I'm tempted if only to shut my brain off for a while, to stop watching every little thing Al does in front of me, likely to drive me mad on purpose.

I turn to Gen. Her hand slips between my legs and grazes my cock through my pants.

There is a world where I can pretend I actually like Gen. Tonight will be the first test.

"Fine," I say and Gen beams at me. "Let me just—"

There's a cry from the billiards room. A thud. Someone screaming. A pool ball knocks to the floor.

What the fuck?

Alice is on her feet in an instant and trailing behind me.

Shadows pass over the blurry glass walls of the billiards room and I catch sight of one with misty edges, one that moves too quickly to be human.

More screams echo out through the walls. The rest of the Joker's Den is watching now, listening.

I know what's happening. I don't know how it's happening or why, but I know none of it is good.

"Everyone out!" I shout.

Comor and the Bonebreakers start ushering people toward the door. They follow orders without asking questions and people start filing out into the night.

"Vane?" Gen calls. "What's happening?"

I snap my fingers at Tin. "Get her out of here."

"What?" Gen's mouth drops open. "Why? What is going on?"

Alice falls into step beside me. Her face is pale, her eyes wide. She knows what this means.

The door to the billiards room slams open and the Captain of the Guard barrels for the exit.

"Fuck," I mutter. I turn to Alice.

"Go," she says, knowing that this must be contained. No witnesses. That's always been our code. "I can bring Roc down."

I give her a nod and push through the panicking crowd with just one goal in mind: kill the guard to contain our secret. Nothing is more important than that.

Sixteen

Alice

In Wonderland, you learn at an early age that you must always be wary around jabberwockies and if you should come across one that has shifted, you have just a few seconds, and fewer tools, to protect yourself from being devoured.

The first thing is caution and the second thing is mercury.

And though I've lived the last four years in close quarters with two of the most powerful jabberwockies, I always make sure I have a vial of mercury on me at all times. Like the royal family, I keep a vial strung from a silver chain around my neck.

Yanking the vial off the chain with a hard pull, I make my way back to the billiards room.

I give the cracked door a nudge.

There are three pendant lights in the room, hanging from chain attached to the ceiling. Two of them have been smashed, casting deeper pockets of shadow around the room.

In the back corner, I spot Roc in his jabberwocky form. All dark shadows and mist and glowing yellow eyes.

I step over the threshold, careful to make no sudden movements.

Once I'm inside, I nudge the door closed with my boot. We can't risk Roc escaping and terrorizing the Umbrage or Darkland at large. It's already gone too far.

What have I done?

I just wanted to frighten Gen, to prove to her she was in over her head. Vane is good at catching himself before the turn. But that moment before the shift happens is terrifying on a good day, enough to scare a spoiled, narcissistic heiress.

It was supposed to be Vane. Not Roc. It was supposed to be Vane's watch.

The room is empty save for Roc. I don't know how many people he was in here with, but I know for a fact he was entertaining the Captain of the Guard and the royal princess.

Only the guard made it out.

Which means...

"Roc."

His silhouette has no shape. It's just dark mist.

"It's me."

I hold up my left hand while keeping my right slightly behind me, the vial of mercury safely tucked in my palm.

Mercury is like poison to jabberwockies. If they ingest it, it will subdue them. If used on them directly, it burns. The problem with using it on a jabberwocky that's already shifted is that their body exists on another plane. It's neither here nor there. More of a nightmare cloud than a body with substance.

If I can get close enough to him, though, I can splash it like acid and it should be enough to pull him back into his body.

I edge around the pool table, hoping like hell he doesn't go in the opposite direction. He'll be faster than me and if he gets to the door before I do, I may not win this fight.

I take another step and his form vibrates, several ripples running through his mist like a rock dropped into a well.

Another step.

He pulls to the opposite direction, backtracking to the opposite side of the pool table.

I freeze.

"I just want to help you."

I've only had to deal with Roc shifting one other time and I had Vane by my side to help. When I asked him later if he remembered what we said, or if he was cognizant of his surroundings while being in his monster form, Roc's answer was, "In a sense." But he left it at that.

When Roc goes still again, I take another step.

He mirrors me, moving in the other direction. Now the pool table is between us and he's closer to the door than I am.

I can't let him get away. His entire existence is at risk because of me. And it wasn't even about him.

This entire time, Roc has always had my back. He's taken my side when he could have easily taken Vane's. Not because he was being difficult but because it was the right thing to do. He always does the right thing.

Until now.

Because of me.

I summon all of the energy I have and lunge forward.

He darts away.

"Shit. Roc!" I climb on the table, race down its length, tear off the cap on the vial of mercury, and leap after him.

There's a monstrous roar, the smell of burning flesh and something deeper, like ichor, like death.

A plume of dark mist clouds around me and then suddenly Roc is corporeal, and we crash together to the floor.

He's a tangle of limbs, his clothing torn, his face and hands covered in blood and gore. There are three lacerations across his face where the mercury singed the skin and muscle.

"Roc. Roc!" I scramble around him, righting him on his back.

His chest rises and falls with breath and checking his neck, I find a pulse.

"Thank god." I sit back on my butt, heart racing in my ears.

This is the fallback of a jabberwocky shifting—they devour everything in front of them, and then when they shift back, they're comatose. Sometimes it's a few hours, sometimes a day or two. At the worst, it's a week. But Vane and Roc are old enough now that he'll likely be out for at most a few days.

Just enough time for us to clean up this mess.

But how the fuck are we going to explain away the disappearance of a Lorne princess?

Tears burn in my eyes.

I prop myself up against the wall and draw my knees into my chest.

"I'm so sorry," I whisper.

Roc didn't deserve this. And now we're all going to suffer the consequences of my actions.

SEVENTEEN

ALICE

VANE RETURNS A FEW HOURS LATER. BY THEN, I'VE got Roc's pocket watch in my hand, the time corrected.

There are dark circles beneath Vane's eyes. His face is puffy and shiny with sweat. His hair too is damp and hanging in his face. Blood is splattered over his shirt and dried and crusted on his hands.

He finds us still in the billiards room.

Roc hasn't moved, hasn't uttered a single sound. He's too heavy for me to move on my own, so I've just sat here with him, quietly watching over him while the guilt and shame festers like a wound deep down in my chest.

"Did you find the guard?" I ask.

Vane comes over to my side and drops down to the floor with me. He spreads his legs out and lights a cigarette.

"Yes," he answers, and some relief ebbs in.

"Did you kill him?"

He passes me the cigarette after he takes a hit. "Yes."

Hands still shaky, I grab the offering from him and inhale deeply.

At least there's that. At least there are no eyewitnesses. It's our word against theirs, and there have been rumors about the princess fucking her guard. We could spin a story that they ran off together. We all saw them leave.

Except at least half the Joker's Den would have known Roc was in the billiards room with the guard and the princess. And how do we explain away the chaos?

"Now what?" I exhale smoke and give Vane the cigarette.

"We double down." He lets the cigarette smolder from the confines of his two fingers. "We get our story straight and we make sure we stick to it."

"I'm sorry." The words come out without me thinking of a reason. They tremble with regret and rasp with my guilt.

"What do you have to be sorry for? It's his fucking fault. He clearly wasn't watching his time and—"

Oh god. He's going to blame Roc. I should tell him. I should fess up.

"We've all been distracted," I hear myself saying.

Just tell him.

Accept the consequences.

"And he's been under a lot of stress."

Vane snorts and takes a draw from the cigarette. "Haven't we all."

We sit in silence for several long minutes, passing the last of the cigarette between us.

Out in the main room of the Den, sunlight is starting to spill in through the front windows.

"We should get him upstairs," Vane says. "Clean him up as best we can and bury the evidence."

Vane climbs to his feet and offers me his hand and hoists me up beside him.

I grit my teeth and try not to cry.

"Thank you, Al."
I lick my lips.
"You're the only one I trust to help me with this."
Oh god.
I can't do this.
I—
"And I'm sorry..." he goes on. "About everything."
I nod, numb, tears burning in my eyes.
There is nothing I can say to fix this.
I've made my bed. Now I have to lie in it.

Eighteen

Alice

We get Roc up the stairs and into his bed. While Vane strips his brother of the bloody, torn clothes, I grab a bowl of hot water and a rag. I start with Roc's face, wiping off the blood from his mouth, from his neck. Thankfully his clothing got the most of it around his torso, so I only have to clean up a few splatters on his stomach. It takes me longer on his nails where blood and gore is packed beneath his fingernails. I have to use a dry brush to get the rest of it.

When we're done, Roc just looks like he spent the night drinking and is sleeping off the effects.

Vane and I, on the other hand, are a wreck.

We take a shower together to help make sure we're sufficiently clean.

He's slow on my hair, scrubbing it from root to tip. He rinses out the shampoo, then gently runs conditioner through it as the water patters down my front.

"I'm sorry I didn't tell you about the engagement."

The tears come out of nowhere. I lean forward, hiding in the stream of water.

"I should have, after everything we've been through."

I don't want to talk about any of this. I don't want to be reminded of what I've done and what I will lose.

Vane and I have always been willing to bury ourselves in each other to forget the pain of the present, the haunting memories of the past.

And so, I find myself turning around and wrapping my arms around him, instinct driving me to the one place where I've found comfort, even if it's existed alongside disorder.

I kiss him.

He lets me.

He sinks his arms to my hips, his hands sliding down to my ass.

The kiss deepens, our tongues meeting, the intensity igniting.

His cock thickens, prodding at my pussy.

I just want to escape.

I want to pretend before it all pops like a bubble.

I reach between us, fisting him in the cuff of my hand.

He groans into me, the sound reverberating deep in his chest.

Rocking his hips forward to meet me, I stroke him, feeling him harden even more beneath my attention.

For the majority of my time with the Madd brothers, this was always what I was chasing. The ability to get lost in Vane and the thrill of him desiring me.

I am distantly aware that this is likely the last time I will have him.

When precum turns him slick, I let go of him.

"Fuck me," I say. "One last time."

He hoists me up into his arms and I wrap my legs around his hips, lining myself up.

The water patters around us.

He presses me into the cool stone wall of the shower and angles his hips, his cock finding me slick for him.

"I'm not giving you up," he tells me and then shoves inside of me.

A mewling sound escapes me but Vane swallows it with his mouth, kissing me with an intensity that sends a thrill right down to my toes.

His pace picks up, chasing the pleasure.

I press my back into the stone, pushing forward at just the right angle so every thrust of his cock builds friction against my clit.

Pressure builds. I'm throbbing and soaked and all of my problems are so very far away.

I don't ever want this to end and yet I'm desperate to come, to release the tension swelling inside of me.

Vane pulls back a fraction and shoves two of his fingers into my mouth. I suck on him, watching him watch me, his gaze hungry and glinting. When he's satisfied, he drops his hand between us, swirling the wet pads of his fingers over my clit.

The pressure sharpens and I approach the edge.

I've fucked Vane so many times that I know when he's close. All the muscle in his back tenses up, his abs constrict, and his rhythm finds a punishing pace.

We don't have to speak. We don't have to warn each other.

We understand each other in a way I've seldom felt.

I come loudly and quickly, pleasure pounding through my body, nerve endings flaring like stars.

Vane pitches forward, groaning into my neck, his teeth grazing my flesh with a nip.

I jolt beneath him, but he captures me, forces me to stay open to him as he pulls out, thrusts back inside, spilling himself at my center.

When we're done, we stay like that panting into one another.

Immediately, the high of the pleasure is tainted by the stain of reality.

Vane sets me down. I swipe a wet lock of hair out of my face as he steps into the spray of water and rinses off.

"I should have just let you go."

He turns his head, the water flattening his hair on his forehead and little rivers following the hollow planes of his face. "What?"

"You and I, Vane, we're…" I close my eyes and try to make sense of all the things crowding in my head. The fear, the regret, the guilt, the hope, the dread and the temptation.

"We were always going to break one another," I say.

His lips part, ready to argue, but then he flattens his mouth and breathes out through his nose and says nothing more.

NINETEEN

Roc

When I wake, it's like clawing out of a fever dream.

Everything is foggy and very far away.

What day is it?

What time is it?

I shove back the sheet and climb out of bed. Beyond the walls of my room, I can hear the beating of two hearts, the inhale and exhale of breath, a pencil lead scrawling across a page.

A jabberwocky has heightened senses on a good day, but after a feast? They are incomparable.

I come out of the room and Vane and Alice look up at me from the table by the windows. There's a plate beside Alice with a half-eaten sandwich. She has a notebook open in front of her, her hand wrapped around a glass of Summerland whisky. Across from her, Vane is kicked back, his boots propped on the opposite chair, a cigarette burning between his knuckles.

They look tired and stressed.

"You're awake," Vane says.

"How long?" I ask.

I'm positive I ran out of time sometime around midnight. Right now the sky is a soft shade of blue with the last rays of orange sunlight just glancing off the rooftops across the street.

"Less than twenty-four hours," Vane answers.

I exhale, relieved. So, I didn't miss too much.

"Was it contained?"

Alice sets down her pencil. "We think so."

"Who was in the billiards room with you?" Vane asks.

I drop into the chair next to Alice. She shoves the plate toward me and I gladly take up the half-eaten sandwich.

Even though it happened just the night before, the memories are distant and hazy, and I can't be sure all of them are real.

I try to place myself back in the Joker's Den in the billiards room. I can see the Captain of the Princess's Guard across the table from me, lining up a shot.

I can see two of his lower ranking men behind him, chatting and drinking and smoking.

There's another woman in the corner holding a leather bag and a glass for—

The Lorne princess.

I look across the table at Vane, mid-chew.

His mouth is closed, his jaw tensing.

"The princess...did she escape?"

"No," he answers.

My stomach rolls. The bread and ham suddenly taste like ash on my tongue.

I devoured a princess. And not just any princess, but the princess of the family my own father tried to overthrow. They'll see this as another act of aggression. Another bit of proof that we cannot be trusted.

There has always been a disconnect between me and the

monster. What the monster does feels like someone else's life. I don't often remember the screams, the taste of their blood. So, it's always been easy to pretend I am absolved of the guilt of what the monster devours.

But not this time.

This time, the consequences will be dire.

How the fuck did I miss the time? I remember looking at my pocket watch and thinking I had an entire hour to spare.

Vane stubs out his cigarette. "Who did you devour first?"

"Probably the princess," I answer. "She was nearest me."

"Then?"

"The lower-ranking guards, but the captain ran."

"I killed him," Vane confirms.

"And the girl?"

Vane and Alice meet with a look.

"What girl?" Alice asks.

"The princess's lady-in-waiting. I can't remember her name...I don't think I devoured her...did you..."

Vane's teeth grit harder. "No. She must have slipped out before we saw her."

"Fuck," I say.

Vane lurches away from the table. "I can still contain this. I can bribe her. Threaten her. She'll keep her mouth shut—"

A floor below, at the front of the Joker's Den, there's a sudden pounding on the door.

We all look at one another.

"Out the back door," I say, and we start gathering our things in a rush.

Alice grabs her hat, then her boots. I grab the first shirt I can find and slip into it. Vane grabs his pocket watch, then tosses me mine.

We hurry down the stairs in a line.

The pounding sounds again, the door rattling on its hinges.

We slip through the backroom and then emerge from the Joker's Den in the alley running behind it.

But we don't make it far.

The Crown Prince is there with a dozen of his guards. They all have guns trained on us.

Normally, I wouldn't be worried—guns are useless against us.

But just behind the prince, partially hidden by the line of his broad shoulders, is Callista, the palace witch, former Heart Witch of the Wonderland court.

She knows our secrets.

She knows what will subdue us.

One of the guards steps forward and aims. When he pulls the trigger, the pop of the bullet echoes off the surrounding buildings.

It hits me in the shoulder.

Pain lances through me.

I've been shot before. A dozen times. But those were normal bullets shot from normal guns.

I smell the mercury first, then comes the eye-splitting pain.

I'm on my knees in an instant, clutching at the gaping wound where blood and liquid mercury leak from me in rivulets.

They shoot Vane next. He gets a bullet in the thigh and goes down hard on the cobblestone.

They don't shoot Alice, but a guard stalks forward and whacks her with the butt of his gun and she collapses next to us, blood gushing from her face.

Well, now...

I think we're well and truly fucked.

TWENTY

ALICE

WHEN I COME TO, I'M LYING ON THE COLD cobblestone in the alley behind the Joker's Den. The wind has picked up and the chill in the air tells me it's probably well into evening.

Voices sound somewhere off to my left. No one I immediately recognize. Both male.

I keep my eyes closed and my body still, listening.

"What kind of monsters are they?" the one guy says. "What kind of beast is subdued by mercury bullets?"

"Have no clue," the other guy says. His accent is more northern Winterland with soft constants and stilted speech.

"You really think they ate the princess? I mean, gross right?"

"They leave no trace of her. Seems odd."

"Yeah. True. Maybe they're holding her hostage?"

"Unlikely," the other man says. "The witch cast a blood spell. The princess is poof. Gone."

A blood spell. Of course, Callista pulled out all her tricks.

Heart witches from Wonderland are experts in spells and magic of the body. But she's claimed to only be a healer for the palace, that she put aside any of her more complex spell work.

I suppose when a princess goes missing, your self-imposed restrictions no longer apply.

"I overheard them talking about looking for the Madd brothers' little sister. An eye for an eye."

Fear lances through me.

Not Lainey.

Please god not Lainey.

The brothers have done an excellent job at hiding her. She's nearby so they can keep an eye on her and visit when time allows, but far enough away from the city that no one would find her unless they knew where to look. We're always careful not to take a cab or carriage directly there. Our routes there are always long and meandering to further shield her.

But with the Lorne princess gone...the rest of the family will likely stop at nothing to find Lainey, if revenge is really their goal.

I have to get to her. I don't sense Vane and Roc nearby, which means the guards took them. Probably they're being tortured right now for answers.

The only person to warn Lainey is me.

I open my eyes a sliver, just enough so I can see the men and the rest of the alley.

It seems like we're the only three here. They've probably been tasked with watching me until I wake up.

Thankfully, it's dark enough in the alley that I'm partially in shadow. But it won't be easy to slip away unnoticed.

The taller of the men fights with a lighter, trying to light a cigarette.

"Let me help," the other guard says, cupping his hands around the flame.

When the men are distracted, I slowly, carefully resituate

myself so my hands are free. And as I shift just slightly, something hard presses against my rib cage on my left side.

My hat. *Yes*. Thank god I grabbed it before we fled.

Now, if I can just get it out and on my head.

The lighter flame gutters out again and the guard curses.

"Turn away from the wind," the other says and they do, putting their backs to me.

Move. Now.

I shimmy the hat out of my jacket, trying to remain as quiet as I can. I hear the roll of the lighter wheel, the snap of a spark.

I bring the hat up and yank it snuggly on my head, and a second later I'm gone.

I keep the hat on as I leave the Umbrage. I run from the Joker's Den further north, past Fortune's Lane and past the High Chamber Council and past the royal palace grounds that stretches from the sea to the center of the island.

When I'm well out of the city, I take the hat off and my body reorients itself on the visible plane.

I huff out a breath.

It's getting late and I'm far outside the city where cabs are fewer and farther between.

I could run all the way there, but it would take me three times as long and I don't know how much time we have. If they find out where Lainey is, their horses, built for speed and stamina, will outpace any cab I can hail.

I keep walking through the countryside until I get closer to the seaside village where all the aristocrats and nobility have summer cottages on the sea.

I spot a cab on the outskirts of the village and manage to hail him.

"I need to get to the Highlands. Can you take me?"

"It'll cost you."

I dig into my pocket and find a handful of coins. "Here. Take it all. Go as fast as you can."

He happily takes my offering and ushers me inside.

The carriage is simple, but swift and we get to the borderland of the Highlands in record time.

I hop out of the cab and start running down the main street through the village, then over the rolling hills outside the village, and finally to the cottage.

When I burst inside, Lainey is in the kitchen at the worktable kneading dough and Ms. Ollen is washing dishes. Both women let out a yelp of surprise and I can only imagine how I look. Sweaty, bloody, and slightly deranged.

"Alice," Lainey says, her hands going still. "What's going on? What happened? Are you hurt?"

"You have to go. We have to go. Right now."

"What? Where?"

I start rummaging in the cupboards looking for a bag. What do we pack? Where do we go? Is here safer than somewhere deeper in the highlands? Tears are burning in my eyes. Panic welling in my chest.

I don't know what to do.

This is all my fault.

What the fuck have I done?

I find a bag and start stuffing things inside of it while Lainey trails me.

"Where is Roc and Vane?" she asks.

"I don't know," I admit. "But...it's bad. They were...shot."

"Shot?!"

"Roc devoured someone he shouldn't have and I think they want revenge."

"Why would he do that?"

I stop rummaging in a closet and finally face her. When

she sees the wetness welling in my eyes, she frowns and puts her hands on my shoulders. "Tell me what happened, Alice."

"I did a bad thing." My voice trembles.

"What did you do?"

The sound of horses fills the night.

"Oh god." I toss the bag and run to one of the front windows and peek through the curtains.

There are seven horses pulling to a stop in the driveway. Callista is on one.

Ice cold realization fills my veins.

I press my fingers to my forehead where the skin is split open, blood now dried on my skin.

You need blood to do a blood spell to locate someone. Of course they didn't have Lainey's blood.

But they had mine.

And I led them here.

I led them straight to Lainey.

I yank the hat out. "I'm going to put this on you. Your uncle made it for me. It'll make you invisible. Do not make a sound."

"But—"

Voices are shouting, growing closer to the house.

"Not a sound. No matter what they say or do. Promise me."

"Alice—"

I place the hat on her head and yank it down low over her forehead and a second later, she's gone.

Twenty-One

ALICE

THEY DON'T BOTHER KNOCKING.

The door bursts open and slams into the wall, the glass pane rattling in its frame.

Callista is first inside followed by several of the higher-ranking guards of the Lorne Palace.

I swallow and step back.

Since Madd made me that hat years ago, I've been the only one to use it. No one really even knows it's magical. So up until now, I've never had the chance to see what it feels like to be in the same room as someone who is invisible.

I can sense Lainey almost like she's one of the spirits that haunt me near the full moons.

She isn't solid. I can't see her. But I can feel her. And I swear I can hear her breathing.

And if I can hear her...

Callista steps forward. "I wanted to believe you were smarter than this, but then I remembered you're a spade. I shouldn't have been surprised."

A lump forms in my throat.

She's right though. I should have been smarter than this. I keep making all of the wrong decisions.

"What do you want, Calli?" I ask, pretending I don't already know.

"Where is she?"

The guards fan out and disappear down the hall, down to the basement, up to the second floor.

All while Lainey hides in plain sight just behind me in the corner of the kitchen.

"We just want some insurance," Callista goes on. "Just until we can get to the bottom of this. We're missing a princess. I'm sure you know how serious that is."

I hear an intake of breath behind me.

Callista follows the sound, her gaze skittering over my shoulder.

I don't move. Don't dare betray what I'm trying desperately to hide.

"Alice," Callista says as she edges around the worktable. "Vane and Roc can't weasel their way out of this one. Help us and I can help you."

"I don't want your help."

I steel myself for whatever comes my way. I owe it to Vane, Roc, and Lainey. I'll give my life to protect her.

Callista takes another step. I want to position myself better, so I'm between her and Lainey, but the movement would be too obvious, so I root myself to the floor.

"You know, I told the royal family they shouldn't trust the Madd brothers. Not only because of what they are, but because of the company they keep."

I swallow as my heart races in my ears.

"Never trust a spade from Wonderland, I told them."

She steps into me, draws a blade from a hidden sheath, and

points the tip at my throat, running me back until I hit the opposite counter.

A breath gusts out of me.

Callista watches my face, scanning my expression, deciding something.

Lainey remains hidden.

One of the guards returns to the kitchen. "All clear," he says.

Callista nods and removes the blade from my throat. She glances absently at Ms. Ollen on the other side of the kitchen, wringing her hands in front of her.

"I see how it is now." Callista smiles, pivots, and throws the blade across the kitchen.

The dagger sails through the air right at Ms. Ollen.

"No!" Lainey shouts, tearing the hat off and popping back into sight just as the older woman catches the dagger mid-air.

Ms. Ollen, the sixty-something-year-old woman, holds the dagger by the hilt, the blade pointing at her face.

Lainey breathes out. "How did—"

"Run!" the older woman shouts and spins the blade around, lobbing it back at Callista.

The witch is fast, and grabs a nearby pan, lifting it like a shield so that the blade clatters into it and clangs to the floor.

"Go, Lainey!" I shove her toward the back door and out into the night.

She starts running to the south, back toward town. Several of the guards spill from the house, close on our trail.

We race across the rolling hills until the village's light comes into view.

"To the cemetery!" I shout because it's the best chance we have. It's not a full moon and I barely have control over my power, but maybe if I dig deep enough, I can summon something to stop Callista and the guards.

At the edge of the village, Lainey veers left, cutting across the main road and winding around the little shops. The cemetery is just beyond the blacksmith, beneath the giant oak tree. It's not as big as Wolbridge, but it'll have to do.

The arched wrought iron gate rises up in the darkness. A single lantern hangs from a post just outside of it, the flame flickering in the breeze.

The thudding footsteps of the guards grow closer.

But just a few feet from the entrance, my knees buckle.

It's been a very long time since I felt the effects of Wonderland magic. It's not the same as the magic in the Seven Isles. Wonderland magic is headier. Wonderland magic makes your ears ring and your vision spark.

I sway.

Lainey stops when she hears me fall. She turns back to grab me. Her mouth is moving, but I can't hear her words over the loudness in my head.

Get up.

Get up.

Everything is heavy. Like my veins are full of lead and my bones full of sand.

Callista circles around to my field of vision.

Several guards grab Lainey, capturing her between their meaty hands.

My tongue goes numb. My mouth dry. I pitch to the left and the ground rushes up to grab me.

Out of the darkness emerges both of the Lorne Princes. They are pale in the waning moonlight, eyes hollow, faces grim.

"An eye for an eye," Crown Prince Evren says, but his voice is far away, like I'm underwater.

"Alice!" Lainey shouts.

And then everything goes dark again.

Twenty-Two

Alice

The chill finds me first, creeping into my fingertips.

My face is wet, mashed into the dewy grass.

When I open my eyes, Lainey is sitting beside me.

"You're here," I mutter, my tongue thick.

She smiles down at me.

"Are you okay?"

Body aching, I slowly sit upright.

In the graveyard, the giant oak sways in the wind, the boughs creaking.

"The princes..." I shove damp hair out of my face. "The guards." I scan the hillside, the cemetery. "Where did they go?"

Lainey's smile falls.

My heartbeat is a slow drum as my stomach sinks.

"Lainey?"

Her chin trembles.

"What happened?"

I crawl over the grass to her and reach out—

And my hand goes right through her.

"No."

Her mouth moves, but no words come out.

"No. No."

The wind shifts again and she shimmers like a mirage.

"No!"

I lurch to my feet and run across the hills, race back to the house.

The door stands open, the house dark and still.

I hurry through the kitchen, into the living room and—

Vane and Roc.

Blood everywhere.

And Lainey in their arms.

Her clothing is torn. Her eyes are wide open and dead.

All of the air is sucked out of the room, and I collapse, unable to breathe.

Roc is holding her close to his chest and sobbing.

Vane's eyes are glassy and faraway, but he's shaking like he's fevered.

I spin around and vomit.

The purging of my stomach and my soul is so deep, my body contorts, heaving until there's nothing left.

My eyes burn.

My throat is raw.

Lainey is dead.

And it's all my fault.

TWENTY-THREE

VANE

DEATH COMES FOR US ALL. A FACT THAT CANNOT BE argued. Both my mother and father are dead. I have stood over their corpses shoved into velvet-lined boxes while a string quartet played in the background and a crowd of mourners murmured their condolences.

I am familiar with death. And I thought I was above it. Because losing my parents didn't break me. No matter how many people came by and shook my hand and tried to hug me, who told me the grief would fade and I would heal, I couldn't summon the right amount of heartbreak to understand what it was they were saying.

My mother had been ill most of her life. A side effect of marrying and birthing monsters, no doubt.

And my father betrayed everything we were.

Did I feel the loss of them? Yes. Did I grieve them? Not really.

So, I thought I was immune to the trauma of death.

But I forgot one very important thing.

Love.

Deep down, I didn't love my parents.

But Lainey...

I haven't moved in five days.

I am hollow.

I can't seem to summon the energy to act like I'm alive when my sister is dead and all I want is to be dead with her.

Everything hurts, including my soul. It hurts in a way I didn't think possible.

But festering beneath the hurt is rage. And I think it's the rage that is keeping my heart beating and my lungs expanding.

It's there, the fury, just simmering beneath the surface.

I pour Roc and myself a fresh glass of bourbon. There is an ashtray on the table between us, full of stubbed-out cigarettes. We've been semi-drunk for the last several days. We've barely spoken. What the fuck is there to say?

How did this happen?

We are so careful with our time.

As boys, our father hammered into us the most important precept:

Do not murder the time lest you devour everything in your wake.

It essentially means that we are meant to keep time alive beside us, honor it, and nurture it like a god. Because without the time, we can't control our monstrous insides.

How did Roc let time slip away? How could he be so reckless?

Maybe we are more like our father than either of us wants to admit.

"I'm sorry," he says quietly, almost like he's been reading my mind.

The question has been running through my head for days.

So, I suppose the answering of it without me asking is no surprise.

"I know," I answer and drown my rage in the bourbon.

The fuzzier I get, the less it hurts. I may just spend the rest of my life drunk.

Our sister was all we had.

Everything good about us.

Gone.

A breath stutters up my throat and I swallow it down, bite back the tears that are always threatening to overtake me.

"I'm going to kill them," I hear myself saying.

Roc stretches out his legs, propping them on the chair beside him. "How? They know what we are. They had mercury-filled bullets. We're fucked."

I light another cigarette. "I'll find a way."

A door opens further in the apartment.

Alice emerges from her room.

We've barely seen her in the days since—

A lump wedges in my throat.

When I think of Lainey too closely, I see her lying in a pool of her own blood.

What they did to her—

My eyes well up again and I sniff them back.

Alice is pale. Bedraggled. Somehow, in just a few days, she seems to have lost several pounds, making her more gaunt than usual. Her face is splotchy, her eyes bloodshot, as if the only thing she's done is cry.

"The funeral is tomorrow," I tell her. "You should shower."

She steps forward, her gaze cast to the floor. She won't look at us.

"I'm going after her."

"Who?" Roc says.

Alice finally looks up. "Lainey."

Roc and I share a look.

Alice is one of the few spades from Wonderland who has control over the dead. Though control is giving her too much credit. She can raise corpses from the ground, mostly only on full moons, and usually only for an hour at most. Sometimes I think she can hear the dead too, because she'll get this vacant look on her face like she's listening to something only she can hear.

But bring someone back from the dead?

Impossible.

"There is nothing to go after," Roc reminds her. "Lainey is dead, and I don't really want to see my sister as a walking dead corpse."

She licks her lips. A tear spills over her eyelid and runs down the globe of her cheek. "Lainey has Wonderland blood in her veins. Which means when her spirit passed over, it went to the Underland."

I snort. "Are you mad?"

"I saw her." Her mouth is a trembling line.

"You think you saw her."

"No. I saw her, Vane. I know I did."

"You had just been knocked out by the butt of a gun, Al and then knocked out again by blood magic. You were probably concussed."

"You're not listening to me."

I shove my chair back and lurch to my feet. "You're not listening to me. There is no Underland. There is no afterlife for us. When we die, that's it. We're gone. Our sister is dead. She's not coming back!"

Alice blinks rapidly and a river of tears streams down her face.

She says nothing to my outburst. She just nods and walks away.

I look over at Roc. "Say something. Was I wrong?"

His eyes are heavy. He's still splayed out between two chairs at the dining room table.

"Lainey is dead." He sets his feet to the floor and slowly gets up. "And nothing will change that. You were right to talk some sense into Alice. That's not hope. It's delusion. And I'm not going to pretend otherwise."

TWENTY-FOUR

ALICE

WHEN JADE SEES ME ON HER DOORSTEP, SHE PULLS the door in and comes out on the stoop, wrapping me in a hug. I want to sink into her kindness, but I don't deserve it, so I give her a half-hearted embrace.

"I need your help," I tell her.

"Of course." She steps back and ushers me inside.

Jade's apartment is on the second floor of one of the Needle Harbor brownstones, so immediately when you walk in, floor-to-ceiling windows give a perfect view of the ocean.

"What do you need?" Jade asks and drops into one of the side chairs in front of the windows.

I take the chair beside her. "I need a card."

She frowns at me.

Most of us displaced from Wonderland don't talk about the cards anymore. We have no reason to. Their power is only good on the other side of the glass.

But there is one thing they do on this side, the one thing I need.

"Why?" she asks, the suspicion clear in her voice.

"I'm going back."

"No, you're not."

"Yes, I am. I can't stay here. I—"

Jade leans forward. "What is it?"

"There's something I never told you. I never told anyone."

"Okay."

"And it might sound crazy."

She blows out a breath. "Half of what we do is crazy."

"When I was ten years old, I managed to collect a full court of cards." I fold my hands in my lap as my fingers tingle. It's been years since then, but I still remember the way my body felt displaced, like I was neither solid nor real. More spirit than living. "I don't know if it's something only a spade can do, but...when I had the full court—a diamond queen, a club, a spade, and a heart—and I went to the looking glass in the Palace of Spades, it opened for me."

Jade's eyes widen.

"I went to the Underland."

She takes this in for several long beats, her gaze faraway.

"You're sure?"

"Yes." I wring my hands together. "I have to go back, Jade. I have to get Lainey back."

"Is that even possible?"

"I don't know. But I have to try."

"You won't know what you're returning to."

"I know."

"The Queen of Hearts could have you killed."

"I know."

"Or worse, maybe there's nothing to return to."

"I know that too."

"If you think this is a way to win Vane—"

"No," I stop her before she can go on. "It's not that. He

and I are done. I can never...he, *I mean we*...it's over. But I owe it to Lainey. And to Roc and Vane."

"To risk your life?"

"Yes." There's that familiar burning in my sinuses again. "My life and more."

"Al—"

"Please, Jade."

She inhales. "You're sure?"

"Yes."

She gets up and disappears into her bedroom. When she returns a minute later, she's carrying a court card. The queen of diamonds. In Wonderland, court cards act like keys. To doors, to realms, to magic, to power. The queens are the most powerful and act, in a way, like skeleton keys, giving the bearer access to it all.

I'm aware of the importance of this act, even if Jade never planned to return to our home world.

"Thank you," I say as she hands it over.

The card is warm and when I shift it in my grip, the hearts reflect the light shining in through the windows.

"How are you going to get the rest of the court?" Jade asks.

"I'm hoping Salty is feeling generous."

Jade laughs. "He'll drive a high price."

"I figured."

She turns serious. "But the heart?"

I stand up and make my way to the door. I don't want to waste any more time.

"The heart will be harder. But she deserves what she gets."

"Callista," Jade says and I nod.

"Just be careful."

I give her a hug. I made Jade's place my first stop because I think I needed some hope. Or maybe I knew deep down she would never deny me a card, and now that the queen of hearts is in my hands, there's no backing down.

I'm all in now.

Twenty-Five

ALICE

JADE INFORMS ME IT'S SALTY'S DAY OFF AND SINCE the Joker's Den is still closed, I find him at his second favorite bar—The Bee Hive. It's not as popular as the Joker's Den, so the crowd is thinner and quieter. The Hive specializes in honey wine, so no one is smashingly drunk. It's more of a sipping crowd.

When I ask Salty for a card, he makes a show of being affronted.

I came prepared, of course.

I pull my hat out of my jacket.

"This was made for me by the Madd Hatter. You can have it in exchange for a card."

He narrows his eyes at me. "*Thee* Madd Hatter?"

"Yes."

Salty knows the name, of course. Everyone from Wonderland knows of the Madd Hatter. But he doesn't know my history with Madd. He doesn't know that at one point, I would have taken a bullet for him.

"What's it do?" Salty asks.

"Makes you invisible."

His eyebrows lurch up. "For real?"

"Yes. You want to make your way up the rank in command," I say, "this will do it and quickly."

"I don't disagree, but once someone higher up finds out what it can do, they'll confiscate it."

I shake my head. "It can't be taken. It must be given."

"Shut the fuck up."

"Try to take it from me." I keep my hands loosely on the brim.

Salty examines the hat, then scans my face for any kind of deception. Deciding he likes the odds, he reaches across the table and tries to take the hat from me. Instead, he gets a sharp zap of pain.

"Shit." He yanks his hand back, shaking it out. "That will happen every time?"

"Yes."

"If I'm being honest, that hat has more value than one of my cards because I don't plan on ever going back to Wonderland."

"There's value in the card for me. I consider it an even exchange."

He nods. "Okay. But I don't understand why you'd want to go back. You don't even know what you're returning to."

"Jade said the same thing."

"Yeah, well, she has a point."

"My reasons are my own."

He turns his glass of honey wine, toying with it as he asks, "This have anything to do with what happened to Lainey?"

"Of course it does."

He nods and reaches into his jacket, pulling out a hand-stitched leather wallet. In an inner pocket, he retrieves a card —a queen of clubs.

He sets it on the table between us. Like Jade's card, Salty's queen shimmers beneath the light. "It's yours," he says. "Free to take."

"I need the hat for one more day."

He sits back in his chair, hands folded over his stomach. "You can take the card. I trust you."

A pang of sadness hits me. At one point, I questioned whether or not Salty could be trusted simply because he worked for the royal family. But it turns out I am the one who cannot be trusted.

"Keep your queen until tomorrow."

"All right." He slips the card back in his wallet.

"But I have one more favor to ask."

He waits.

"I need you to get me inside the palace."

There is one more card to obtain, but before I can get it, I need to make one more stop.

I find Nix still lingering at Kenny's. They're both in the kitchen while Kenny's shop girl runs the front. Kenny is melting chocolate in a pot while Nix samples the day's freshly baked goods.

"I have a question for you," I say.

Nix says, "Oh yeah?" around a mouthful of chocolate donut.

"Did you really come here on a job?"

He smiles at me, swallows. "Nah. I'm on vacation."

"I knew it."

"Even assassins need rest."

Kenny rolls her eyes from her place by the stove.

"Do you feel like taking on a job?"

Nix licks chocolate frosting from the end of his finger.

"Maybe. Depends on who it is and the price you're willing to pay."

One of the benefits of living with the Madd brothers that I am eternally grateful for is that they've never charged me rent. Which means all of the money I've earned over the past few years has been saved.

I set two fae gold bars on the worktable.

Nix pauses his licking and eyes the metal gleaming beneath the pendant lights.

"That's a lot of money."

"I know."

"Who do you want me to kill? The king?"

"Close."

He raises a brow.

"A witch."

"Alice," Kenny says, an air of reproach in her voice.

"Let the adults barter," Nix says, keeping his gaze on me.

"I have a way inside the palace and a method to conceal your movements. I just need you to back me up if I get into a spot of trouble, but my priority is the witch. I want her dead."

Nix sweeps up the gold with quick, deft fingers. "You have yourself a deal."

Twenty-Six

Alice

Salty comes through on his promise and is able to slip me into the palace through a staff door on the northeast side of the building. From there, he gives me clear instructions on how to reach Callista's private quarters and how best to avoid the guards.

The Darkland palace was constructed in the neo-noir style with jutting buttresses and soaring turrets and stone gargoyles perched at the roofline. It's one of my favorite buildings in all of Darkland.

I've rarely had the opportunity to be inside—once for a charity ball, and once for a wedding of a lesser noble, someone Vane and Roc were related to.

Any event held at the palace is hosted in the ballroom, where no expense was spared on the elegant boldness of the decorating and the architecture. Here, on the other side of the building, saved mostly for servants, the walls are gray plaster, the millwork plain wood. All expenses *were* spared here, even the lighting system. The halls are dark, the windows fewer and farther between.

I get up to the third floor easily and pass only a few servant girls who are busy going about their tasks.

Callista's rooms are in the southern wing. When I come to her closed door, I stall, realizing I didn't think this part through. Do I just barge in? What if the door is locked? I don't know how to pick a lock.

I lift my fist and give the door a sharp rap.

"Come in," Callista calls absently.

I suppose the most obvious strategy is sometimes the best one.

I push the door in. It opens on a short hallway that then opens to a sitting room. Callista has repurposed hers to be both a sitting room and a workroom. On the left, two black velvet chairs around a fireplace, and to the right, floating shelves and a long cabinet, the top full of work instruments, stacked books, hand-labeled jars and bowls.

Callista is at the counter grinding something down in a mortar with a stone pestle.

When she spots me, the grinding stops, the pestle going still.

I'm the last person she expected to enter the room.

She slowly sets the bowl down, then places her hand on the countertop.

"What do you want?"

It does not escape me that just a foot away from her fingertips lies a sharp dagger.

"I need your queen of hearts."

I may have surprised her by walking through the door, but I have not surprised her with this request.

She adjusts her weight, shifting from one foot to the other. The movement puts her hand several inches closer to the blade.

"You're trying to go back," she states.

"Yes."

"Why?"

There's a soft parting of air behind me.

"Lainey was innocent. She didn't deserve to die."

"And you think Rosalind did?"

"I didn't say that. But even if I had, Rosalind likely felt no pain. Did you see what they did to Lainey?" My voice catches.

Callista purses her lips. "You of all people know there is no such thing as mercy or fairness when power is at stake."

"It's my fault though." The confession is out before I can think better of it.

"What do you mean?"

What difference does it make if I tell her my secrets? I don't plan for Callista to walk out of here and Nix would never judge me. If I speak them aloud, then maybe there will be some respite from the guilt gnawing at my insides.

"I wound back Roc's clock on accident. It was supposed to be Vane."

Callista's mouth parts in shock. "He didn't do it on purpose?"

"No."

"Why do it at all?"

"I just wanted to scare Gen."

She laughs, but I can tell it's mocking. "You are your own worst enemy, you know that, don't you?"

Of course I do.

"Let me make this right."

"You can't. You can't bring back Rosalind. And now Vane and Roc will be banished for good. There is no way for them to dig themselves out now."

I breathe in deeply, trying to quell the rising well of anger and shame. I'm not going to pretend that what happened to Rosalind and what happened to Lainey was the same. I'm not here to argue about the cause, the consequences, or the results.

"I'm going back," I say. "I only need a heart card."

She drums her fingers on the counter. "You can't have it." The dagger is now a foot within reach. Is she a good throw? Can she send it sailing right for me, killing me where I stand? And if so, how long do I have?

"I thought you might say as much."

I'm just about to give Nix the signal to act, but the door bursts open behind us and Vane steps in.

Fuck.

What is he doing here?

"I'm popular today," Callista says.

Vane ignores the witch and looks right at me. "Whatever you think you're doing, don't."

"Vane..." His name comes out sounding like a plea.

"Walk out this door with me, Al." He glances at Callista, his teeth grinding together. "They'll get what's coming to them."

"Ohhh a threat," Callista says.

"I can't," I tell him.

"Al—"

"She can't," Callista cuts in, "because the guilt and the shame will not let her."

Vane's expression falls. He glances between me and Callista, deciding.

"What's she talking about?"

My eyes are growing blurry before I've gotten a word out. But I can't tell him. I can't admit it to him and then see the realization, the betrayal bleed into his face.

"Please leave," I tell him.

"Alice. Tell me right now."

"Ask yourself," Callista says, "how the infamous Madd brothers would be so careless as to let time run out on the night of a very public celebration, of all nights."

Vane's gaze cuts to me. He doesn't have the truth yet, but I can see the questions are starting to mount.

"After all," the witch goes on, "who was the one person losing everything that night? It wasn't Roc. Not by a long shot." She moves away from the cabinet. "Who was the one who might want a little chaos in the name of revenge?"

"No," he says.

The tears are spilling over now. I can't stop them even if I wanted to.

"Al, tell me she's lying."

I swipe at the tears. My voice is thick when I say, "I can't."

Vane's eyes flash yellow right before he lunges at me.

Twenty-Seven

Alice

I pull the vial of mercury from around my neck and uncork the bottle as Vane slams into me.

My feet go out from beneath me and we fly back into one of the chairs beside the fireplace.

The momentum and Vane's size has us careening over the chair and slamming to the stone floor.

I don't have time to uncork the vial.

There is never time to spare with a jabberwocky.

I bring my arm up and smash the bottle against his temple.

The glass shatters, shards cutting into the palm of my hand. Liquid silver shimmers in the light.

Vane scrambles back, writhing.

I get up on my feet just in time to see Callista running toward me, the dagger in her hand.

She's just feet away from pouncing on me when someone barrels into her, sending her flying sideways.

Nix has appeared, my hat in his hands.

"Get him contained," he directs me and turns back to the witch.

I race to Callista's worktable and start rummaging through the jars. Dragonwood. Mugroot. Fae blood. Siren scales.

Mercury.

The bottle is big enough to fill a dozen vials.

Nix and Callista slam into a nearby end table. She starts speaking in *mervay*, a Wonderland language used for magic. Nix clamps his hand over her mouth, cutting off the words as he sinks his own blade into her throat.

With Vane still writhing on the floor, I uncap the bottle and start casting a circle around him.

The shimmering silver beads on the stone floor. Vane tries to swipe for me, but his vision is likely blurred, his senses diminished, and I'm easily able to dodge him.

Within seconds, the circle is complete.

The vapor barrier is invisible, odorless, but to Vane, it's not only poisonous like it is for the rest of us but immediately debilitating. He won't be able to cross the perimeter for hours.

His breathing grows labored, his body shaking.

I stagger back.

Callista thuds to the floor.

On all fours, Vane slowly turns his head so he can look at me.

"I'm going to kill you."

I nod. "I know."

"I'm going to get out of this circle, Al, and I'm going to kill you. I'm going to wrap my hands around your throat and squeeze the air from your lungs until your face turns blue."

I'm sobbing now.

"And just when you're about to leave this plane, I'm going to let you take a breath just so I can do it all over again."

I blink rapidly, trying not to let his words, his promises, his pain get to me. I deserve all of it. All of the violence and the suffering.

If I could take it all back, I would. But I can't. I can only bear the brunt of his anger and hope that I can follow through with my own promises.

Nix appears beside me, his bloody fingers holding the queen of hearts.

"As promised," he says.

I take it from him.

Vane manages to straighten, rocking back on his knees. He's pale, a sickly green color. "And I'm going to kill you too."

"I'm always up for a challenge," Nix says.

"We should go." I slip the card into my pocket and retrieve my hat.

"If I were you, I'd run as far and as fast as I could!" Vane shouts.

At the door, I turn back. His eyes are burning bright yellow.

"I'm going to get her back," I promise him. "If it's the last thing I do."

Twenty-Eight

Days Later

Roc

At the end of an alley, just off Wilcox Avenue on the northwest end of the Umbrage, sits a warehouse. Tucked in the back of the warehouse is a full-sized looking glass with an ornate gilded frame.

Vane and I stand in front of it now, our reflections looking back.

We were just children when we left Wonderland and came through this glass. Now we are broken men.

Vane lights a cigarette. I fall back into an old wooden chair and pull out a flask, taking a long swig.

"Do you think he'll come?" Vane asks as he snaps his lighter closed with a flick of his wrist.

"Lainey was his favorite," I say. "He'll come."

But we wait. We wait for hours.

Just before sunset, when the light is both sharp and dull, the door opens.

The warehouse is long and narrow, with several bookcases

up front, and aisles and aisles of stacked crates and draped furniture.

We hear his steps first. There is a slow, lazy gait to him, as if he is never in a hurry to get where he's going, as if he and time are disconnected.

When he comes around a shelf and into the fading light of day, he stops, takes a drag on a cigarette rolled in black paper.

He always did love his novicii cigarellos. The smoke smells sweet and spicy, like licorice and cloves.

A black velvet low-top hat sits on his head, dark hair sticking out from beneath the brim. Trapped behind the silk band circling the crown of the hat is a Wonderland wild card —the only one in existence.

"We weren't sure you'd come," Vane says.

Our uncle steps forward and comes to a stop in front of the looking glass. He says nothing and takes another pull on his cigarello. Smoke curls in the light spilling through the nearest window.

It's been a while since I've seen Uncle Madd, better known as the Madd Hatter. But nothing about him has changed. He still looks roughly the same age, mid-thirties now. In truth, he's probably several hundred years old. He's the older brother to our father and while dear old dad never told us his exact age, he implied on several occasions that he was older than the Age of Spades which took place two and a half centuries ago.

"We think she went through just a few days ago," I say.

"She take the hat?" he asks.

For as long as I've known Alice, she's kept the eight-piece hat close but always refused to wear it. I had suspected our uncle had made it for her. It wasn't until Vane told me it had invisibility powers that my suspicions were confirmed. All this time, she had a hat that gave her the power to eavesdrop whenever she liked. It's made me question everything I've ever said.

It doesn't excuse what she did, but it certainly makes more sense now that I have more context. I'm almost positive she was in the alley the night she and Vane had an altercation in the Joker's Den. She was always brash, reckless. She likely heard Vane dismissing her importance and decided to take it out on us. Why she fucked with my watch and not his, I will never know. But it doesn't fucking matter now. What's done is done.

"She left the palace with the hat in hand," Vane answers.

"Rumor has it a palace guard now owns it," I say.

"We think she bartered it for a card," Vane adds. "So, it's likely it's on this side."

Uncle Madd nods. He captures the cigarello between the bite of his teeth and then reaches out for the mirror. When his fingers touch the glass, it ripples like water.

He grabs the cigarello and exhales. When the smoke hits the mirror, it bounces back, the glass solid again.

"You really want her dead?" he asks.

"Lainey is gone because of Al," I say, my voice catching. "She deserves whatever she gets."

"Make her suffer," Vane adds. "Make it hurt."

Madd laughs, a low rumble in his chest. "When I catch her, she'll beg for death."

He drops the cigarello, exhales a breath of smoke and steps through the glass.

Epilogue
A Lifetime Later

The boy is seven years old.

He is alone in one of the many rooms at the palace. His parents are in the next room discussing the planning of another ball meant to be hosted on the palace grounds. He can't remember what they're celebrating this time. Something about alliances between Darkland and Neverland.

He's playing with his toys, a wooden rabbit and a tin fae with wings, gifted to him by his uncles.

Well, they aren't his uncles by blood, but he's spent enough time with them that the blood doesn't matter to him one bit. They treat him like family and that's all that matters. The constant presents don't hurt either. All of his uncles love to shower him with gifts.

At this point in his imaginative battle, the rabbit is losing. The rabbit always loses.

In the other room, he can hear his father telling his other father that the ball should feature a signature drink, a combination of rum and bourbon. They'll call it Seven Isle Iced Tea.

"Everyone will be drunk by sundown," is the rebuttal.

"Yes, but imagine how smooth it'll go down," is the reply.

In front of the boy, in the corner of the room, stands a full-length mirror. The mirror itself is suspended on two arms attached to the base, so that a person can angle the mirror up or down.

For as long as the boy can remember, the mirror has stood there, though no one ever uses it. It's almost like it's art or a relic. When he was very small, barely walking, he can remember toddling near the mirror only to be swept up by his father. "Never touch it," his father had told him. "Don't go near it."

"I don't want the entire party inebriated," his mother says. "Maybe we make them small glasses? Sipping drinks?"

His father sighs. "Fine, fine. Whatever our Darling wants, our Darling gets."

The mirror lets out a squeak, the glass tilting.

The boy looks up.

The mirror pivots again, angling down.

The battle between rabbit and fae is forgotten and the boy gets up.

Another squeak.

The base jitters on the hardwood floor.

When the boy is close enough to see his reflection, the glass ripples, distorting his face.

And then a hand pokes through.

And the hand is followed by an arm, then a leg.

The boy steps back as a girl steps through.

The boy has seen a great many magical things in his life. Men with wings. Women who fly without wings. Men who glow. Women who make things appear and men who make things disappear.

But he's never seen a girl step through a mirror.

She scans the room. It takes her a few seconds to realize he's there as he's half her size. She is tall, but slight, maybe close to his mother's age, if he had to guess.

"Where am I?" she asks.

The woman is dark-haired and scarred like a soldier. Her bare arms are tattooed from fingertips to shoulders. Even her neck is tattooed with several black and grey roses twining around a gothic blade.

"The palace," the boy answers.

"Darkland?" she asks.

"Yeah."

"Do you know the Devourer of Men?"

The boy has heard the nickname a hundred times before.

"Yes."

"Where is he?"

The boy turns away from the woman and crosses the room. "This way."

The woman follows.

The boy shoves open the pocket doors and steps into the next room where his two dads are at the bar and his mom on the settee.

They've never made the distinction of which father is his, but everyone knows because he looks just like his blood father, black-haired, green-eyed, sharp like the devil.

And if his features did not make it obvious, his early craving for blood would have.

"Daddy," he says.

His father, the King of Darkland, the Devourer of Men, looks over at him. "What is it, Lanon?"

"A lady came through the mirror. She asked for you."

His father is suddenly rigid.

His other father, Captain Hook, is racing to his side to scoop him up.

"Get him out—"

The woman steps into the room.

"Roc," she says. "It's me."

In all the years of his life, the boy has considered his father a vision of control. He will laugh and he will joke and sometimes he will even anger. But he has never seen his father disarmed.

He has never seen his father cry.

"Lainey," he says. It's not a question. It trembles, instead, with years and years and decades of withering hope. "Is that really you?"

"Yes," she answers and crosses the room in an instant and wraps her arms around the boy's father.

And the man, known as the Crocodile, the Devourer of Men, wide-eyed and stunned, breathes her in and collapses against her and sobs.

I did not intend to write this epilogue in the beginning. I thought we'd end with Vane, Roc, and the Madd Hatter at the looking glass, Alice's (and Lainey's) future TBD.

But I saw this boy playing with his toys in front of the mirror and a woman walking through, and I couldn't shake that image, because I knew what it meant. So I wrote it. Truth be told, I thought Alice's series (upcoming, someday, I don't know when *don't hate me*) would be about saving Lainey, but the more I thought about it, the less excited I became. Because while there is redemption for Alice in bringing Lainey back, ultimately Alice's journey is about her own power, her major character flaws, and how to live with both and I didn't want to cage it within the framework of saving Lainey. In a way, I worried the goal of saving her would distract from the journey Alice needed to go on. And yes, yes, she will definitely go on that journey with the Madd Hatter! Cue the major enemies-to-lovers vibes.

This book isn't like my other books — for one, there is no romance! But writing it was a bummer and a joy because I could let Alice be as dark, and as flawed, as she needed to be, just like the men I write. Women make mistakes too. Big, life-altering mistakes. Sometimes, the worst kind. I hope you enjoy this one for what it is — a woman in her detriment, learning how to become something else despite the darkness she lives with.

If you want to stay up-to-date on news of Alice's story (or any other books!), subscribe to my substack (it's free!):

https://nikkistcrowe.substack.com/

Also by Nikki St. Crowe

DEVOURER DUOLOGY

Devourer of Men

Devour the Dark

Dark & Darker Still: A Vane and Roc Origin Story

VICIOUS LOST BOYS SERIES

The Never King

The Dark One

Their Vicious Darling

The Fae Princes

WRATH & RAIN TRILOGY

Ruthless Demon King

Sinful Demon King

Vengeful Demon King

Wrath & Reign Omnibus

HOUSE ROMAN

A Dark Vampire Curse

MIDNIGHT HARBOR

Hot Vampire Next Door: Season One

Hot Vampire Next Door: Season Two

Hot Vampire Next Door: Season Three

Hot Vampire Next Door: Season Four

Hot Vampire Next Door: Season Five

Secrets Drenched in Blood: Midnight Harbor Omnibus

BONUS SCENE ANTHOLOGY

Ink & Feathers

About the Author

Nikki St. Crowe is a *USA Today* Bestselling Author of several romantasy novels, including the #1 Amazon Bestselling Series, *Vicious Lost Boys*.

When not writing about villains getting the girl, and the girl getting the power, Nikki can be found with her husband and daughter on the shores of Lake Michigan hunting for the perfect sunset.

Visit Nikki on the web at:
www.nikkistcrowe.com

Nikki's Substack:
https://nikkistcrowe.substack.com/

instagram.com/nikkistcrowe

amazon.com/author/nikkistcrowe

threads.com/@nikkistcrowe

bookbub.com/profile/nikki-st-crowe

* 9 7 8 1 9 5 9 3 4 4 3 5 3 *